Macarons and Mayhem

A Peridale Cafe MYSTERY

AGATHA FROST

For questions and comments about this book, please contact
pinktreepublishing@gmail.com

www.pinktreepublishing.com
www.agathafrost.com

Edited by Keri Lierman
Proofread by Karen Sellers and Eve Curwen

ISBN: 9781521927830
Imprint: Independently published

Other books in the Peridale Café Series

A
Peridale Cafe
MYSTERY

Book Seven

CHAPTER 1

"T his is *hopeless*!" Barker exclaimed as he forced a fork through the butter and sugar. "Maybe I should leave the baking to you, Julia?"

Julia smiled softly as she pried the fork from his firm grip. She added the eggs and then picked up the electric mixer. Barker examined the forming batter, flour on the end of his nose. Julia chuckled as she dusted it off.

"If I can teach Jessie, I can teach anyone," Julia said as she passed the mixer to Barker. "It's all in the wrist action. You need to fluff it up so the air doesn't escape."

Jessie looked up from her tablet and smiled smugly across the kitchen. Julia had not let Barker know there was a five-pound bet relying on her teaching him how to successfully bake a Victoria sponge cake before the end of the day. From the look on Jessie's face as she tapped on the tablet screen, she was already spending her winnings.

Barker whizzed the machine around the mixture, a crease forming on his brow, his tongue poking out of the side of his mouth. Julia thought he looked adorable.

Julia's talent and passion had been passed down from her mother, but she was not sure if she could pass it onto Barker. Julia and Barker had been in a relationship for six months, and it had taken nearly all of those months for Barker to agree to the baking lesson. He paused to wipe the sweat from his brow with the edge of his apron, smearing self-raising flour across half of his face.

"Is this right?" he asked with an arched eyebrow as he performed an unnatural movement with his wrist, sending a blob flying across the kitchen in the process. "I think I'm getting it!"

"*Erm*," Julia mumbled as she tried to adjust Barker's wrist to no avail. "You're getting *better*."

"He couldn't get any *worse*," Jessie mumbled, humour clear in her voice. "Even *I* wasn't *this* bad. I can't believe I'm missing my driving lesson for this."

Julia shot a stern look across the kitchen to her seventeen-year-old lodger and apprentice as she gave Barker's shoulder a reassuring squeeze. Jessie had not been the easiest student, mainly because she had not liked being told what to do, but even she had picked it up quite easily. Julia looked over at the pile of deflated and burnt cakes with jam and cream seeping out of their middles. She wondered if this was the best use of her Sunday afternoon.

"Let's add in the flour," Julia said, pulling the mixer from his grip to replace it with a metal spoon. "The trick is to fold it in so it doesn't flatten the cake. We need to keep as much of that air that you just mixed in as possible."

Barker began to carefully fold in the flour, a little better than he had the previous times. Julia wondered if this might be the one to succeed and actually rise in the oven.

"Add a drop of vanilla extract into the mix, and then you can grease the sandwich tins," Julia said, giving up her hopes of Barker getting the batter any smoother. "Then you're ready to bake again."

Barker unscrewed the vanilla extract bottle with trembling fingers, glancing at Julia for reassurance. She gave him an encouraging nod and watched nervously, hoping he had learned what a '*drop*' meant after almost pouring a full bottle of the flavouring into his last attempt. To her surprise, Barker added just a splash of the extract. He stepped back as though to restrain himself, then screwed the small bronze lid back onto the bottle. Julia let out a relieved sigh.

"Imagine if the boys at the station could see me now," Barker said with a nervous laugh as he brushed down the ill-fitting floral apron. "I don't think they would ever listen to me as their detective inspector again. Didn't you have any aprons that weren't so girly?"

"Of course," Julia said.

"We thought you'd look pretty in the floral one," Jessie added. "Brings out your eyes."

Barker removed the lid from the butter dish with pursed lips and stabbed the greasing brush into the golden butter. He quickly covered the two sandwich tins, seeming to remember what Julia had said about making sure to get every inch evenly coated, so the greaseproof paper had something to stick to.

Without Julia's assistance, Barker traced the bottom of the tin onto the paper twice before sloppily cutting out the circles. Julia would have done it as close to the edge of the paper instead of the middle like Barker had, but she bit her tongue, not wanting to hamper his progress. He roughly placed them into the bottoms of the greased tins before cutting out pieces for the sides.

"*Perfect!*" Barker exclaimed with a firm nod as he clapped his hands together. "I think this *might* be good enough to sell in your café, what do you think –"

Barker's voice trailed off when Julia's grey Maine Coon, Mowgli, jumped onto the counter, and with one swift bat of his paw, sent the mixing bowl flying to the kitchen floor. Julia clenched her eyes and sighed as she listened to the batter splattering across her tiles.

"*Mowgli!*" Barker cried. "You little *sneak!* It's all over my briefcase!"

Mowgli scurried across the counter, knocking as many things over as he could before diving through the open window and into the bright garden. Jessie chuckled behind her fingers as Barker wiped the mixture off his briefcase. Knowing when to give in, Julia twisted the oven dial to off and pulled off her apron.

"We'll try again next weekend," Julia said, pulling a crisp five-pound note from her purse. She tucked it into Jessie's hand without Barker seeing. "Clean yourself up. I'll sort out this mess."

Barker tugged his apron over his head, sprinkling flour on his dark brown hair. His defeat tormenting him, he plodded off to the bathroom, looking as though he wanted to curl up in shame.

"Lost cause," Jessie said with an air of authority as she held the shiny note up to the light of the window. "He'll never learn."

"This one wasn't his fault," Julia said as she picked up the bowl from the floor before tossing it into the sink. "I only gave in because I couldn't see any more of my ingredients going to waste. I *will* teach him."

"Put another fiver on it?" Jessie asked as she tucked her winnings into the pocket of her black hoody. "You might make me a very wealthy girl if we keep playing this game."

Julia shook her head with a smile, leaving Jessie to get back to her device. She quickly wiped up the mess on the floor, cleared away the ingredients, and put all the utensils into the sink for washing later. She paused and brushed her finger along Sue's pregnancy scan picture stuck to the fridge. Butterflies fluttered giddily in Julia's stomach every time she looked at the twins she was soon going to be an auntie to.

When the counters were sparkling again, she picked up Barker's briefcase and put it carefully on the side of the counter. She wiped a damp cloth over the glistening leather, making sure to run it along the seam with her fingernail. She crouched down and stared at the pale mixture she had missed. It looked like it had seeped inside. The lock combinations were both set to '*000*'. Julia clicked the two small buttons, and the top popped open.

She wiped away the tiny slither of batter that had managed to leak inside the case. She had not intended to read the piece of paper on top of the stack, but she was unable to help herself when her eyes wandered over her own name in the mass of black text. Before she could read anymore, Barker returned from the bathroom, swooped in, and snapped the briefcase shut.

"Some of the mixture got inside," Julia said defensively as she tucked her curls behind her ears. "You've kept your combination as '*000*'?"

"It's easy to remember," Barker said, his cheeks turning a deep shade of crimson. "Were you reading what was in there?"

"I saw my name."

"It's nothing."

"Nothing with *my* name on it?" Julia asked, folding her arms across her chest. "What is it?"

"*Nothing*," he mumbled, his cheek colour deepening as he put the briefcase behind his back. "Fancy a cuppa?"

"Not until you tell me why my name is in your briefcase," Julia said with a small laugh as she reached around Barker's back. "Is it police paperwork?"

"No," he said, lifting the briefcase above his head and out of Julia's reach. "Just forget it."

"You can keep saying that, Barker old boy, but it won't wash with her," Jessie announced without looking up. "Cake Lady is like a dog with a bone when she gets a sniff of something."

Before either of them could reply, knuckles rattled against the front door. Barker appeared relieved, but the distraction only irritated Julia. Jessie was right about Julia being a dog with a bone; it bothered her not knowing what Barker was hiding from her. She relented and walked around him, casting a final glance at the leather briefcase before turning into the hall.

"Alright, *alright*," Julia called out as she hurried towards the door, the knuckles continuing to rap on the frosted windowpane. "Where's the fire?"

She was surprised to see Emily Burns, her elderly neighbour who lived in the cottage on the other side of the winding country lane. She was sporting an excited grin, with a magazine clutched tightly against her chest.

"Have you *heard?*" Emily asked with a small squeak, her teeth biting her bottom lip as she stared expectantly at Julia. "Have you heard the good news?"

"I'm not religious, Emily."

"Not *that* good news," Emily said with a chuckle as she turned the magazine around. "This is even better than that! *Here*, turn to page six."

Emily thrust a copy of *Cotswold Gardening Magazine* into her hands. Julia looked down at the beautiful azaleas on the cover, concealing behind a pleasant smile that she had never heard of the publication. She turned to page six all the same.

"What am I looking at?" Julia asked as she scanned the page, which was titled '*Local News*'.

"Right *there*," Emily said, jabbing a finger above

a small block of text in the margin. "Oh, *Julia*! It's *marvellous* news!"

Julia squinted at the tiny words under Emily's finger in the bottom right-hand corner of the magazine, trying to remember the last time she had been to the opticians to have her thirty-seven-year-old eyes tested.

"'*Cotswold Gardening Magazine is pleased to announce that our next issue's featured location will be the small picturesque village of Peridale*,'" Julia read aloud. "That sounds fun."

"It's *more* than fun!" Emily exclaimed. "*Cotswold Gardening Magazine* is coming here! To *our* little village! They're going to take pictures of our gardens and interview the villagers, but that's not the best part!"

"There's more?" Julia asked, trying to feign excitement for a topic she did not care much about. She looked around her modest patch of land, which was neat and regularly weeded, but nothing compared to the beauty of Emily's rose garden across the lane, which she tended to daily.

"They're going to be holding a competition, and the best garden in Peridale will win *ten thousand pounds*!" Emily exclaimed as she took the magazine back and clutched it to her chest once more. "Now that *I'm* president of the Peridale Green Fingers Club, that money is as good as mine!"

Emily proudly adjusted a small enamel leaf pin on her blouse, her spine suddenly straightening and her chin poking up in the air.

"*Congratulations!*" Julia exclaimed, not wanting to admit she had no idea such a club existed in the village. "That's great news."

"Yes, I suppose it is," Emily agreed with an uncertain smile, her eyes dropping to the ground as her excitement faded for the first time since knocking on Julia's door. "Although I wish this pin had been handed to me under better circumstances. Our previous president, Yolanda Turner, crashed her car last month and she didn't walk away to tell the tale."

"Oh, that's awful," Julia said, her hand drifting up to her mouth. "I'm sorry to hear that."

"Yes," Emily said with a firm nod. "We can't dwell on the past though. Our village is about to become famous, Julia! We're going to be in a magazine! *A magazine!* It's going to mean more business for your café. Once the rest of the Cotswolds sees how beautiful our little corner is, they'll all want to experience it for themselves. *Must dash!* I need to plant new flowers right this second.

The judges are coming this week to decide which locations they are going to shoot."

Emily hurried down the garden path with her magazine, scurried across the lane, and burst back into her cottage. Julia laughed to herself as she closed the door behind her. Nothing in Peridale surprised her anymore. She was sure Emily had rushed across to be the first to break the news to Julia before anyone else could. Gossiping and Peridale went hand in hand, and Julia was in no doubt what the conversation in her café tomorrow morning would revolve around.

"What was that about?" Barker asked as he pushed a fresh cup of peppermint and liquorice tea across the counter to Julia.

"Nothing important," Julia said, glancing at the briefcase. "Just something about a gardening magazine coming to Peridale to take some pictures. The way Emily was talking, you would think The Queen herself was paying us a visit."

"Doesn't take much to get this place excited," Jessie said. "You gonna tell us what's in the briefcase, Barker?"

Julia smiled gratefully at Jessie, glad she had been the one to bring up the briefcase. Barker lifted his cup up to his lips, his cheeks blushing again. He took a deep sip before resting the coffee cup against his chest, his eyes darting to the case on the counter. It had not gone unnoticed to Julia that the lock combinations had been scrambled.

"It's honestly nothing," he repeated with a soft smile, his eyes imploring Julia not to push the subject.

She blew on the surface of her hot tea, deciding that she would leave it for now. She wanted to believe that she could ignore the urge to find out why her name was written on a piece of paper in Barker's briefcase, but she knew herself better than that. One way or another, she would find out what he was hiding from her.

CHAPTER 2

Monday mornings in Peridale always felt like an extension of Sunday evening. The village moved slowly, as though not wanting to admit that the weekend was over. It was always the quietest day of the week in Julia's small café, and even though this Monday morning was no exception, she had noticed a certain buzz in the air.

She almost felt foolish for not knowing about

the Peridale Green Fingers, considering it appeared that half of the village were members. Word of the magazine had travelled quickly, and by the time Julia and Jessie drove to work, half of the villagers were already awake and tending to their gardens.

"I don't see the point," Dot, Julia's gran, announced as she sipped her tea from the seat nearest the counter in Julia's café. "It's all a bit *useless*. You plant the bulbs in winter, so they bloom in spring. They look pretty through the summer, but they're shrivelling up and dead by autumn, and then you have to start the whole cycle again in winter. I can find better uses for *my* time!"

"Are you sure the real reason you don't see the point is because you're hopeless at gardening?" Julia asked as she painted the edges of a marzipan flower with a small brush dipped in pink food colouring.

"I don't need to be good at it," Dot said with a dismissive wave of her hand. "I pay Billy's dad, Jeffrey, to cut the grass once a month and I let the rest grow. It's *natural*. How is Billy, Jessie?"

Jessie looked up from the cake display stand she was polishing. Her cheeks flushed, and her eyes narrowed.

"How should *I* know?" she snapped, before picking up the bottle of window cleaner and hurrying into the kitchen.

"*Young love,*" Dot sighed as she stared off into the corner of the room. "I almost can't remember what it feels like."

Julia glanced through the beaded curtain into the kitchen where her young apprentice was checking her phone. Jessie had yet to admit that she was seeing local troublemaker, Billy Matthews, but Jessie did not know Julia had caught them kissing behind the café a couple of weeks ago. Even if she had not caught them, the way Jessie looked at her phone whenever it announced the arrival of a new text message gave everything away. It was the same look Julia found herself giving Barker whenever she saw him.

"How do these look?" Julia asked as she placed the final rose on top of the last cupcake. "I had some free time, so I thought I would make these for the Green Fingers."

Dot cast her eyes over the delicate handcrafted edible flowers of all colours, which lay on top of a dozen lemon buttercream cupcakes. Her tongue poked out of the side of her mouth as her hand reached out for the one adorned with a yellow daffodil. Julia slapped her hand away and secured them under a plastic lid.

Macarons and Mayhem

"How am I supposed to tell you if they're any good?" Dot mumbled through pursed lips. "I can't wait for this whole ordeal to be *over*! The entire village is going flower mad. It's positively driving me up the wall."

"I suppose that means you won't want your garden photographed for the magazine?"

"Well, I never said *that*," Dot said thoughtfully as she sat back in her seat and picked up her small teacup. "It *is* a magazine, Julia. Let's not be hasty."

Julia chuckled as Jessie thrust through the beads, tucking her phone into her jeans pocket. She avoided both of their gazes as she took a bucket of water and a cloth over to the window, which looked out onto the village green.

"Texting anyone interesting?" Dot asked, winking at Julia out of the corner of her eye. "Any *boyfriends*?"

"It was just Dolly and Dom," Jessie snapped back. "They were asking about college stuff."

Even though Dolly and Dom were Jessie's best friends, and the only other people she would be texting, Julia saw the lie written across Jessie's face. The teenager had been living with Julia since the beginning of the year, and she had come to know her like the back of her hand. Whenever Jessie lied, her nostrils flared and her ears twitched, something she had done when answering Dot's question.

"I'm going to pop these into the Green Fingers' meeting," Julia said as she pulled her apron over her curls and dusted down the front of her salmon coloured summer dress. "Emily told me this morning they were meeting in the village hall to discuss the competition."

"Ten thousand pounds for some flowers and grass," Dot whispered bitterly before draining the rest of her tea. "I should go. Some of the girls and I are heading down to London for the evening. Barbara managed to snap up some cheap tickets for *The Lion King* musical, and it would be rude not to. See you later, girls."

"Bye," Julia and Jessie chimed in unison as Dot hurried out of the café, her pleated skirt fluttering behind her.

Julia watched as she darted across the village green, weaving in and out of a game of football a group of boys were playing. The ball headed for her, and instead of dodging it, she kicked it through the goal before adjusting the brooch holding her stiff white blouse collar in place. Julia hoped she had half her gran's energy when she reached her eighties.

Leaving Jessie to look after the café, Julia walked

around the village green with her box of cupcakes. The scent of freshly mown grass tickled her nostrils as the sun prickled her face. She was particularly proud of how the flowers had turned out, considering how tricky they had been to craft. Her mother had always made it look so easy, but it had taken Julia most of her adult life to perfect the skill.

Julia walked past St. Peter's Church and pushed on the door of the more modern village hall, which had been built in the 1970s. It was home to many different clubs and organisations, none of which Julia was a member of. Between running her café and juggling her home life with her relationship, she did not have a spare second to indulge in anything other than a little therapeutic baking.

The hall was brightly lit, with the fluorescent tubes in the low ceiling shining on the polished wood floor beneath. Pine disinfectant and the engrained scent of cigarette smoke hit her as she walked through the door. Seats were arranged in a circle in the middle of the room, but they were all empty. If it was not for Julia's neighbour, Emily Burns, and Amy Clark, the church organist, talking on the other side of the room, Julia might have thought she had heard wrong about the meeting.

She took a step forward, her heels squeaking on

the floor. She waited for Emily or Amy to turn around and acknowledge her, but neither of them looked up. They were talking in hushed whispers, their voices echoing around the vast hall.

"You *mustn't* worry," Emily said through almost gritted teeth. "You're going to *ruin* this for all of us."

"But I feel so *bad!*" Amy pleaded as she stuffed her hands into her pale pink cardigan pockets. "What if *they* find out?"

Julia cleared her throat, not wanting to be caught in the act of eavesdropping. Both elderly women spun around, their heels also squeaking on the floor. They pushed forward wide smiles, but Julia could feel the strain behind them.

"I brought some cupcakes for the meeting," Julia announced, an echo to her voice. "Do I have the right time?"

"You're a little early," Emily said as she walked across the hall, her smile widening. "The slimming club has only just finished. *Oh, Amy!* Would you look at these cupcakes? They're *gorgeous!*"

Joy bloomed within Julia. She poured her heart and soul into everything she baked because she knew it made the result better. If she had no one to share her creations with, it wouldn't be half as fun.

"So *realistic*," Amy added as she joined Emily. "I

bet they taste even better than they look."

Emily nodded, the green pin on her blouse sparkling under the lights. Amy glanced at it, the corners of her smile faltering. Julia almost wanted to ask if everything was okay, but she knew it was not her place. She was not part of the club, and she was not about to become a member, even if there was a cash prize up for grabs. The money would be nice, but she knew she did not deserve it.

Julia walked over to the tables underneath the window. She looked out at the graves in the cemetery, spotting her mother's amongst the mass of stones jutting out of the grass. Her mother had not just been an excellent baker; she had also been a skilled gardener. Julia did not doubt that if she had lived beyond Julia's twelfth birthday that her mother would have been a Green Finger, if not the president of the whole club.

As she was about to excuse herself, a group of villagers walked through the doors, chatting amongst themselves, a shared enthusiastic look of excitement on their faces. Aside from one blonde woman who Julia recognised from her school days, Chloe Johnson, Julia was bringing down the average age by more than several decades.

"Julia baked cupcakes to celebrate the good

news," Emily announced brightly, the tension from earlier either gone or well hidden.

"I foresaw a sweet surprise this morning in the tea leaves!" Evelyn, the eccentric owner of the B&B, announced from the crowd as she pressed a finger to the glittering brooch in the middle of her bright green turban. "I should have known it meant you, Julia!"

The group made their way over to the box, *'ooh'ing'* and *'ah'ing'* as they peered at the small cupcakes. Julia looked around the room, realising she had underestimated how many people were coming to the meeting. She recognised most of the faces, and it seemed that every old age pensioner was in attendance, apart from her gran.

"I must be getting on," Julia said, glancing at the door as more villagers poured into the hall. "The café won't run itself."

"Oh, Julia! This is *wonderful!*" Evelyn exclaimed through a half-full mouth after biting into one of the cakes. "Lemon buttercream? *Inspired!* I didn't need *the sight* to know your baking would be delicious as always!"

"We should have her bake for the prize reveal," Amy suggested. "The magazine is putting on a little show to announce the winner of the best garden in

Peridale, and they've given us a budget to sort out the arrangements."

There was a murmur of agreement as those closest to the cupcakes scooped them up, leaving the rest who didn't get a cake to stare longingly at those who did.

"That settles it," Amy said with a nod. "That's if you want to?"

"I'd be honoured," Julia said, glancing at Emily, knowing she was the president of the club. "If that's okay?"

Emily looked at Amy, apparent rage flaring her nostrils, but she did not let the emotion register on her face for too long. She turned to Julia with a beaming smile and nodded.

"*Of course*!" Emily exclaimed in a singsong voice. "I couldn't think of anyone better."

"The cards told of a new business opportunity in the village!" Evelyn cried, throwing her arms up through her kaftan and pointing them to the roof. "*Praise the heavens*! They never fail us with their all seeing eye."

Julia smiled her thanks, knowing Emily's anger was most likely directed at Amy for stepping on her presidential toes and not directed at Julia's baking.

"Think about what you want, and I'll come up

with some ideas."

"How about *macarons*?" Amy exclaimed, looking around the group for encouragement. "Those little French things. They're so colourful and light! I had them on holiday last year. They were delicious."

The villagers nodded enthusiastically. Julia noticed the same angry flare of Emily's nostrils again.

"*Macarons*?" Julia confirmed with a gulp, not wanting to admit they were the one baked item she had always struggled with. "Consider it done."

Julia left the group to get on with their meeting. She had lived across the lane from Emily for over two years, but it was not until now that she had seen this new side of her. It surprised Julia how seriously she was taking her new position and pin.

On her way out, she spotted Johnny Watson, a journalist from *The Peridale Post*, parking his car behind a Peridale Cleaning Company van. They were the same age, had gone to school together, and had even gone on a date when Julia first moved back to the village after spending her twenties and early thirties living in London with her now ex-husband. The date had only affirmed to Julia how good they were as friends, but Dot and her sister, Sue, still insisted that Johnny had always been in love with her. Julia did not want to think that about Johnny, but she often caught him giving her a similar look to the one Jessie gave to her phone.

Johnny headed in her direction, his face buried in a bundle of papers. He adjusted his glasses, dark circles under his eyes. His usual neat bow tie was messily done, and his short curly hair was dishevelled. He did not look up and spot her until he almost walked straight into her.

"*Julia!*" he cried as he pushed his glasses up his nose. "What are you doing here?"

He looked around her to the door of the village hall. The chatter of the meeting floated through the open windows, Emily's voice rising above the noise. Julia glanced down at the papers in his hand, but she could not quite read them upside down.

"I've just dropped off some cakes to congratulate the Green Fingers," Julia said as she hooked her thumb over her shoulder. "I didn't have you down as the gardening type."

"I'm not," he said rather sternly, his eyes darting down to the papers. "I was just – *actually*, I'm glad I've bumped into you. You were the first person I thought of when the police laughed me out of the door."

"Police?" Julia replied, her ears rapidly pricking

up. She leaned in a little, her arms folding firmly against her chest. "Are you in trouble?"

"I'm not, but I think the Green Fingers are," Johnny said, glancing at the door again. "*Here*, look at these."

Johnny pulled her into the shade of a tall yew tree. He stared down at the papers, biting his lip nervously. It was clear to Julia that he had not slept a wink. He finally turned the papers around and passed them to Julia.

"Obituaries?" Julia asked as she looked over the writing. "I don't understand."

"Margaret Harwood and Elsie Davies," he whispered as he looked around the church yard. "Both died three weeks ago, one day after the other. Both in their seventies, and both fell down the stairs."

"Okay?" Julia replied, not noticing anything unusual in the typical style of obituaries she found in *The Peridale Post*. "Is it uncommon for people of a certain age to trip and fall?"

"No," Johnny said, almost frustrated. "But it *is* uncommon for their obituaries to be sent to the newspaper a day *before* they actually died."

Julia's ears swiftly pricked up again. She looked back at the writing and scanned it once more. Both obituaries detailed their lives and family members. Nothing seemed out of the ordinary.

"Are you sure?" Julia asked as she handed the paper back to Johnny. "When did you last sleep?"

"I *couldn't* sleep," Johnny snapped as he quickly polished his glasses on the edge of his navy-blue shirt. "I discovered this by accident. I was filling in for Rhonda. She usually deals with the obituaries, but she has that bug that has been going around the village, so I started sorting through the paperwork on her desk. I found these last night and matched them to the issue they were published in. Rhonda is thorough, and she dates everything. When I noticed these were dated the day before the date of deaths in the newspaper, I stayed up all night making sure it wasn't a mistake."

"Isn't it?" Julia asked sceptically.

"I wish it were," he whispered, looking her straight in the eyes, his dilated pupils magnified behind his spectacles. "I traced them back to the day they were sent in. Nobody knows where they came from, or who sent them, but they definitely arrived the day before each of these women died."

"And you've shown this to the police?"

"I've just come from there," Johnny said bitterly. "Your *boyfriend* practically pushed me out of the station. Said they were accidents and that Rhonda must have got the dates wrong, but I called Rhonda first thing this morning, and she was sure of the dates because she remembered the first one turning up on her desk on Saturday morning. She ate a curry at The Comfy Corner the night before."

"And they only serve curry on Friday nights," Julia said with a nod. "Spicy Friday."

"Exactly,' Johnny said, a nervous smile flickering across his lips. "That's not all. I was trying to find a connection between Margaret and Elsie, and aside from being women in their seventies, I couldn't find much, except for *one* thing."

"Go on," Julia urged, more than a little intrigued.

"They were both members of the Peridale Green Fingers," he announced triumphantly. "I searched their names in the newspaper database, and by chance, I came across an article I wrote three years ago when the new allotments opened up near Peridale Farm. I interviewed both of them, and they were even in the picture with Yolanda Turner cutting the ribbon."

Julia thought for a moment, wondering if she believed what Johnny was saying, or if he was trying to piece something together that was not there. She considered the alternative for a moment. If he was right, it meant both women had been murdered, and the obituaries had been sent as a twisted joke. Even compared to the mysteries Julia had stumbled upon and solved, this one seemed a little far-fetched.

"Are you going to tell them?" Julia asked, glancing over her shoulder at the village hall. "You might spook them."

"I'm writing an article about the magazine and the competition anyway," he said as he stuffed the papers into the canvas bag looped over his shoulder. "Emily Burns called and told the paper about the news this morning. It won't stop me from asking questions about these deaths if I need to. If somebody *is* targeting the Peridale Green Fingers, I can't just sit back and do nothing."

Julia opened her mouth to talk Johnny down, but she stopped herself. She was certain she had said the exact same words when she had been sure she was onto something. She gave him an encouraging smile, knowing what it felt like to be disbelieved about something so serious.

"If there is anything I can do to help, let me know," Julia assured him with a soft smile. "And promise me you'll get some sleep?"

"Okay," he said dismissively. "Keep your ears

open for their names in your café."

Julia promised that she would before Johnny hurried around her and into the village hall. She had been away from her café longer than expected, so she hurried across the village, pondering everything Johnny had told her. Now that she thought about it, she remembered hearing about two elderly residents dying, but she didn't recall anyone mentioning their deaths being anything other than tragic accidents. They had not been hot topics in her café for long. If there was a mystery there, it was not hers to solve. Breathing a contented sigh of relief, she pushed on the door of her café, a smile infecting her lips when she saw Billy and Jessie chatting at the counter.

"He was just leaving," Jessie mumbled, her eyes dropping to the floor. "Weren't you?"

"Call me, yeah?" Billy said as he walked past Julia. "Missing you already, babe."

"*Shut up*," Jessie whispered, summoning her usual teenage grumble. "Whatever."

The café was quiet, and the stock check and deep clean could wait until tomorrow. Julia made them both a cup of peppermint and liquorice tea, and they sat at the table nearest the counter and talked about everything aside from Billy Matthews.

CHAPTER 3

Despite going to sleep with a clear mind, Julia awoke the next morning with thoughts swimming around her head, all of which revolved around what Johnny had told her.

As she sipped her tea, with her half-eaten slice of wholemeal toast sitting next to her, she scrolled through the web page after searching for '*Margaret Harwood*'. As she had suspected, there were not many results. Like most people over seventy in the village, she did not have much of an online footprint. Aside from her obituary, which detailed her career as a cleaner at St. Peter's Primary School, being widowed three years ago, and leaving behind no children, there was not much else to read about. Her name popped up in a couple of articles connected to the Peridale Green Fingers, but there was nothing online to give Julia any hints about her life aside from the basic facts.

The same could be said for Elsie Davies. She was also widowed but left behind a daughter and three male grandchildren, all of whom were now grown up. She had worked as a secretary at the police station before retiring and spending her time in her garden. She had come third in a competition to find the best jam in Peridale in 2004, petitioned to keep the library open in 2009, and had been included in many Peridale Green Fingers related articles along with Margaret.

Julia clicked on the article about the opening of the allotment Johnny had told her about. Margaret and Elsie were standing side-by-side, next to Yolanda Turner, who was holding a pair of giant gold scissors in front of a green ribbon. Emily and Amy were on the other side with two other men, all beaming at the camera. Julia recognised the men as Edgar Partridge, a retired butcher, and Malcolm Johnson, a recluse with a criminal reputation who lived on the outskirts of the village. The rest of the Green Fingers were on the edges of the photograph, all looking directly down the lens.

Julia slammed the laptop shut and wondered if there really could be something suspicious going on. It was not uncommon for women in their seventies to fall, even if it was unusual for two to die within a day of each other. No matter how much she tried to rationalise their deaths, she kept coming back to the obituaries. If it had not been for them, she might have dismissed things entirely, but she could not seem to explain them in a way that made her feel comfortable.

"You've been researching those deaths, haven't you?" Jessie asked with a yawn after shuffling out of her bedroom. "I thought you said you were going to leave it."

Julia almost denied her lodger's accusations, but Jessie knew her too well. She looked down at the closed laptop and nodded, unsure of what she would have done with any information she might have found.

"Something feels a little off," Julia admitted as

Jessie filled the kettle to make two cups of peppermint and liquorice tea, even though Jessie never finished a full cup. "How did those obituaries get there before those women died?"

"Like you said last night, it's probably just an admin error," Jessie said before letting out a long yawn. "What's in the oven? It smells good."

"Macarons," Julia said with a sigh. She slid off her stool and crouched to peer through the dimly lit oven at the tray of pink macaron shells. "I never know when they're done."

"I thought you were the Goddess of baked goods?" Jessie replied as she poured boiling water into two cups. "You can bake anything."

"Macarons are tricky. They need a steady, low temperature. Too high and they burn, too low and they don't cook all the way through." Julia opened the oven and pulled out the tray. She gave the tops a little prod with her finger, but they didn't have the hard shells she needed. "I'm going to need *weeks* to perfect this."

"I have faith," Jessie said as she handed Julia a cup of tea. "Find anything interesting online?"

"Just the usual," Julia said, taking up her seat at the counter once more. "They weren't the types of women who posted everything on their social profiles. They didn't even *have* social profiles."

"What were you expecting to find?" Jessie asked with an arched brow. "A status update pointing you to a murderer? *'Just been pushed down the stairs. About to die. Will update from the afterlife.'*"

Julia let out a soft chuckle as she blew on the hot surface of the tea. She could always rely on Jessie's dry humour for some perspective.

"Johnny thinks the Green Fingers are being targeted," Julia said as she stared down at Mowgli crunching his cat food. "If they are, it would help to know why."

"It's probably just a coincidence," Jessie said as she put her cup on the counter after taking one sip. "I need to shower. I smell like Mowgli after he's been rolling in the garden."

Jessie shuffled off to the bathroom, the sound of rushing water immediately filling the cottage. As Jessie woke up under the hot water, Julia's mind whirred, trying to piece something together, which could have plausibly been cooked up in Johnny's imagination.

She thought until a light bulb sparked above her head. At the same moment, the shower cut off, and Jessie emerged with a towel tucked under her arms, her wet hair dangling over her face.

"I've had an idea," Julia said nervously, pushing forward a smile. "It *probably* is nothing, but it's better to be sure. If somebody is targeting the Green Fingers, I need to find out why."

"Okay?" Jessie asked as she pushed her hair away from her eyes. "How are you going to do that?"

"I need somebody inside," Julia said with a nod, her smile widening. "Somebody to ask the right questions."

Jessie stared at her for a moment before she realised what Julia was implying. When she did, she laughed awkwardly, shaking her head as she turned to her bedroom.

"Not a chance," Jessie called over her shoulder. "I'm far too young to hang around with those old cronies."

Julia felt deflated for a moment until another light bulb sparked above her head. She sipped her tea with a pleased smile as Jessie dressed for work, knowing exactly who she was going to ask.

***

"YOU WANT ME TO DO *WHAT*?" DOT cried as she thrust an empty beer can into a black bag. "Those damn kids from the Fern Moore Estate need to stop throwing their rubbish into my garden! I bet your boyfriend is one of them, Jessie."

"He's not my boyfriend," Jessie mumbled. "And Billy doesn't even hang around with those guys anymore."

Julia watched as Dot bent over and picked up the last can in her small garden. She was trying to think of the right things to say to convince her, but Dot was stubborn when she wanted to be.

"It will only be temporary," Julia urged, leaning over her gran's garden wall. "And there's a cash prize up for grabs. You never know, you might have a secret talent and scoop up the money."

"I have *many* talents, Julia," Dot said as she straightened up and knotted the bag. "Gardening isn't one of them. Why do you want to start investigating this anyway? I knew Margaret and Elsie. They were old and *clumsy*. Nobody was surprised when they died. They were the best of friends too. I'm not surprised they went together."

"I just have a feeling," Julia said as she chewed the inside of her cheek. "It doesn't matter."

Dot smiled apologetically before looking down at the plastic box Julia was holding. She peered down at the macarons and gave Julia an uneasy look.

"Are they supposed to be so – *wonky*?" Dot

asked tactfully. "I'm sure they taste lovely."

"We're still perfecting the recipe," Jessie answered for her. "Give us a week, and they'll be the best macarons you've ever tasted."

"I've never been much of a fan of them," Dot said with a shrug as she adjusted the brooch under her neck. "French food and I don't mix. The girls wanted me to go to a French restaurant when we were in London yesterday, but I point-blank refused! You won't catch me sucking a snail out of its shell anytime soon!"

"How was *The Lion King* musical?" Jessie asked.

"There was a lot of singing and dancing," Dot said through pursed lips as she pushed her curls up at the back. "Not my cup of tea. I was expecting real lions, not half-naked men in hats, but I suppose if you like that sort of thing – *Oh*! Who's that poking around in front of your café?"

Julia turned and looked across the village green at her small café, which was sandwiched between the post office and the hair salon. A woman and a man were staring at Julia's flower box under the window. The woman scribbled something down on a clipboard while the man took photographs.

"I think they're from the magazine," Julia said as she turned on her heels. "I'll see you later."

Macarons and Mayhem

Julia and Jessie walked across the village green, the August morning sun beaming down on them. Peridale was a beautiful village, but it was at its most attractive during the height of summer. All the flowers were in bloom, the leaves were still green on the trees, and the weather was the best it was going to get all year. She was not surprised the magazine had chosen August to feature Peridale.

Julia approached the man and woman slowly as they talked in low whispers. She pulled her café keys from her pocket to catch their attention.

"You must be the owner of this rather delightful flower box," the woman said, her teeth and tongue wrapping around every letter with perfect enunciation. "It's a rather *brave* choice to have poppies and yellow chrysanthemums side by side, but I dare say it works."

Julia smiled her thanks, even if the handiwork was not her own. She did not admit that she paid a company to tend to her flower boxes to make her café look as inviting as possible.

"You must be the judges from the magazine," Julia said as she held out a hand while balancing the macarons with the other. "I'm Julia South, and this is Jessie. You're both more than welcome to come into our café if you want to sample some of our cakes."

"Best cakes in Peridale," Jessie announced proudly. "Although don't look too closely at these macarons. Bit wonky."

The woman stared down at Jessie with a strained smile. She appeared to be in her early fifties. There was not a black hair out of place in her sharp bob, her make-up was clean and subtle, and her red blazer and pencil skirt were completely free of creases. She exuded effortless grace and authority in a way that made Julia feel uncomfortable. The man, on the other hand, appeared a little more relaxed as he flicked through the pictures he had just taken with his professional camera. He looked to be around Julia's age. He was wearing loose jeans, a baggy t-shirt, had dirty blonde surfer-style hair, and had a goatee beard framing his mouth.

"*Mary!*" Emily Burns called out as she scurried towards them from the direction of the village hall. "*Brendan!* I wondered where you had got to."

"We were just admiring Julia's charming flower boxes," Mary said with a frozen smile. "And her *peculiar* arrangement choices."

"She doesn't do them herself," Emily quipped as she peered down at the clipboard. "She pays somebody to look after them."

Macarons and Mayhem

Julia recoiled, a little taken aback by Emily's blunt confession. Julia did not care that Mary knew she was not a talented gardener, but she had not expected her neighbour to announce her secret to score points. Julia glanced at the pin shining from Emily's blouse and wondered if it had anything to do with Emily's sudden change of character.

"I captured some good shots," Brendan said, his accent distinctly Welsh. "The yellows and reds will really pop in print."

"You're including them in the magazine?" Emily asked, her eyes widening as she forced an uncomfortable smile in Julia's direction. "Why don't I take you on a little tour of the village? I'm dying to show you my roses."

Before any of them could object, Emily pushed herself between the judges and dragged them away from Julia's café and towards the winding lane up to her cottage.

"What's got into her?" Jessie mumbled as Julia unlocked the door. "She's acting like such a weirdo."

"Power," Julia said with a quick wink. "Goes to people's heads."

It was not long before Julia's café was filled with villagers. Julia put her macarons on the counter and offered them to customers for free in return for constructive criticism. Despite their misshapen appearance, their unique flavour seemed to go down well.

"*Macarons*!" Barker announced as he walked into the café on his lunch break, his briefcase in hand. "How cosmopolitan. Haven't seen them since I was in London."

"They're for the grand prize reveal," Julia said as she offered him one. "Between you and me, they're not my finest effort."

Barker took a bite into a rose flavoured macaron. Pink crumbs dropped down his chin and stuck to his shirt as he chewed the light and airy creation.

"It's definitely *floral*," he said with a small cough as he placed the second half back on the counter. "Not my cup of tea."

Julia pulled a piece of chocolate cake from under the counter that she had sliced five minutes ago in preparation for Barker's usual lunchtime visit. His eyes lit up as he leaned in to kiss her.

"Now you're talking," he said rubbing his hands together while licking his lips as he took the seat nearest the counter.

Julia made him his usual black Americano and placed it in front of him as he tucked into the rich, double chocolate fudge cake, not caring about the buttercream all around his mouth.

"I heard Johnny Watson from *The Peridale Post* came to see you," Julia said casually as she arranged the cakes in the display cabinet. "I bumped into him yesterday."

"Total nutcase," Barker said with a roll of his eyes. "Tried to tell me two women were murdered and that their obituaries were sent to the paper as warnings. Didn't have a scrap of real evidence, aside from some woman's guarantee that she was sure of the dates because of a curry night at The Comfy Corner."

"Spicy Friday," Julia corrected him. "You don't think there's anything to it?"

"Do *you*?" Barker asked with a small laugh. "It's a bit unlikely."

"I suppose it is," Julia said, suddenly feeling a little foolish for her early morning research. "You're probably right."

Barker licked his fingers as he finished his cake. He wiped his mouth with the back of his hand before pushing the plate away and leaning back in his chair. Julia couldn't take her eyes away from the briefcase on the floor next to him, the urge to know what was inside rising once more.

"Delicious as always," Barker announced with a

pleased grin. "This magazine visit has turned everyone at the station bonkers. I didn't know so many of them were so interested in gardening. It's all they're talking about."

Julia peered through the window as Emily dragged Mary and Brendan towards St. Peter's Church, bypassing Dot's cottage entirely.

"It's certainly captured the village's attention," Julia mumbled as Emily dragged them both into the village hall. "I just hope people go back to normal when –"

Before Julia could finish her sentence, her mobile phone rang behind the counter. She never put it on silent because the only people who would ever call her while she was at work lived in the village and they were more likely to pop in and visit her than call. She hurried behind the counter and pulled her phone from her handbag, her stomach knotting when she saw Johnny Watson's name flash on the screen.

"*Hello?*" Julia said, waving goodbye to Barker as he headed for the door mouthing that he would see her later. "Is everything okay?"

"No, it's not, Julia," he said, his voice shaking. "Do you know Edgar Partridge?"

"The name rings a bell," Julia said with a nod. "I

think he lives in a cottage near the B&B."

"Is he dead?"

"I don't think so," Julia replied. "Why?"

"Another obituary just came through," he said, his voice small and afraid. "Same as the last one. Just appeared on the desk and nobody knows where it came from. I'm on my way down there now."

"I'm closer," Julia said, already pulling off her apron. "I'll meet you there."

Julia ended the call and tossed her phone back into her bag. Barker had left his briefcase next to his table. She realised it was her chance to find out why her name was written on a piece of paper inside it, but she knew this was more important. She told Jessie to watch the café, then headed straight for the door without a second glance back at the case.

She ran through the village, hurrying past The Plough pub, which buzzed with life, past the police station, and past Evelyn's B&B. There was a small row of cottages at the end of the lane. She knew Edgar used to be a butcher in the village, and she remembered seeing his face at the meeting the day before, as well as in the allotment article photograph. She tried to recall which cottage was his out of the three, but it quickly became clear which it was. Only one of them had an elaborate and beautiful garden worthy of the Green Fingers.

Gulping hard, Julia unclipped the pristine white gate and hurried down the small path, colourful flowers everywhere she looked. She rang the doorbell, the chimes echoing down the hall. There was no answer. She banged her knuckles on the frosted glass, desperately hoping that the door would fly open and everything would be okay.

"*Edgar?*" she cried as she pressed her ear up against the wood. "Are you in there? It's Julia from the café."

Instead of hearing a reply, Julia heard a deep voice cry out, followed by what sounded like something heavy tumbling down the stairs. Julia stepped back, her heart skipping a dreaded beat. Something else thudded down the stairs, forcing Julia to drop to her knees. She pulled back the tricky spring-loaded letterbox to peer into the cottage. She looked through to the kitchen, where the back door was swinging in its frame.

Julia's eyes wandered to the bottom of the stairs, and just as she had feared, a man lay motionless in a heap on the floor. She jumped up, her heart thumping out of control. The panic rose in her, but she forced it down, closing her eyes for a second. She tried the door handle, but it rattled in the lock. With all her strength, she crashed her body into the door, but her small frame was not heavy enough to knock down the thick wood. She stepped back and looked around the garden, her eyes landing on a small gnome with a green hat and fishing rod amongst a bed of lavender. Without a second thought, Julia tossed the small gnome through the door's window, and then reached inside to unlock it.

"*Edgar?*" she whispered as she hurried down the pink-carpeted hallway. "Edgar, are you okay?"

Julia rolled the poor old man over, her hand clasping over her mouth when she saw his vacant eyes staring aimlessly up at the ceiling. There was no denying he was dead.

"*Julia?*" Johnny's voice cried breathlessly from behind her as he stepped over the broken glass. "Is that —"

"We were too late," Julia said with a shaky voice as she stood up and clasped her hand against her forehead. "I knocked on the door, and then I heard him fall, and then —"

She remembered the second thudding down the stairs and the swinging back door. She hopped over Edgar, avoiding looking into his glassy eyes. She yanked on the open back door and stared pointlessly into the lavish green garden. She stepped out into the burning sunlight, the eerie silence unsettling her. Gulping hard, she looked for any movement. A butterfly fluttered past her before landing on a stone sundial, but the garden was otherwise still.

Julia turned back to the cottage and watched as Johnny called the police. Guilt surged up in her chest. How could she have suspected Johnny had imagined things?

She stepped back into the kitchen, suddenly noticing faint pink half-footprints on the black tiles. She looked at the pale pink carpet in the hallway leading up to Edgar's body, but what was on the tiles was a thick liquid. Julia crouched and patted the mysterious pink substance with her forefinger. Rubbing it against her thumb, she lifted it to her nose. She presumed it was paint of some kind, but it had a distinct chemical smell that was strangely familiar to her. Realising it could be evidence, Julia stood up and walked carefully as she made her way to the front of the cottage to wait for the authorities with Johnny.

She no longer doubted the reporter, and she was going to do everything in her power to find out who she had heard flee Edgar's cottage.

CHAPTER 4

J ulia placed a tray of fresh macarons on a table just as Emily walked into the café with Amy trailing behind her. Julia had only invited Emily to sample the macarons, but she was not surprised Amy had tagged along with her; she had been counting on it.

"These look delicious as always, Julia!" Emily announced as she took a seat at the table in the middle of the café. "They will be perfect for the party. We have permission from the council to hold it on the village green to attract as many people as possible. It's all rather exciting, don't you think?"

Amy took a seat at the table next to Emily as Julia prepared a pot of tea. She was not sure if it was her imagination, but Amy appeared distant as she plucked at the bobbles on her pale pink cardigan.

"I must say I was *quite* surprised when your gran asked to join our little club this morning," Emily said as Julia walked over with the tea tray. "I always thought she hated gardening."

"I think the magazine visit has stirred something up in her," Julia said with a smile as she carefully placed the tray next to the plate of colourful macarons. "Help yourself, and be honest. I'm still working on the flavours, so I'm open to criticism."

Julia mulled over her thoughts as Emily and Amy took little bits of each colour, making small comments about how delicious they were. Amy did not suggest any tweaks, but Emily offered suggestions for stronger or subtler flavours. Julia took notes in her small notepad, but her mind was on the notes on the other side of the page that she had scribbled down after being interviewed by the police the previous afternoon.

Macarons and Mayhem

"Quite terrible what happened to Edgar yesterday," Julia dropped in as Emily poured herself a second cup of tea. "I heard he was a member of your club."

"A *founding* member," Amy said, the sadness clear in her voice. "There are not many of us left now."

Julia noticed the little glance Emily shot Amy's way, but Amy was too detached to notice. With her chin poking in the air, Emily poured Amy a cup of tea and added milk and sugar for her.

"Terrible way to go," Emily said. "I'm glad my cottage doesn't have an upstairs. I trip over the rugs enough."

"He was pushed," Julia said. "There's no doubt about that. I was at his cottage when it happened. I heard the murderer run down the stairs before fleeing through the back door. Unfortunately, I didn't see who it was."

"How *dreadful!*" Emily cried dramatically, after taking a small sip of tea, her eyes narrowing to slits. "He was an excellent Green Finger. Beautiful garden."

"Do you have any idea who might have wanted to kill him?" Julia asked, looking past Emily and straight to Amy, who was now furiously fiddling with the sleeves of her woolly cardigan. "Or if he was linked to Margaret and Elsie?"

"Their deaths were *accidents*," Emily answered quickly. "Why should they be connected?"

"Because somebody warned of all three deaths before they happened," Julia said before sipping her own tea. "I thought the deaths were nothing more than accidents until Edgar. Now I am certain the deaths are linked, as are the police."

"Linked how?" Emily asked, her head tilting slightly.

"By *your* club," Julia replied firmly as she leaned forward to rest her elbows on the table. "They were all members of the Green Fingers after all."

"Coincidence, I'm sure," Emily said. "Why would somebody want to target our group? We just grow flowers, for goodness sake."

"They were founding members *too*," Amy mumbled, her eyes widening as she stared blankly at her tea. "There are only three of us left."

"*Two*," Emily corrected her. "Malcolm is no longer a Green Finger."

Emily instantly sat up straight, her face hiding behind her cup as though she had said too much. Julia resisted the urge to flip her notepad to her investigation page so she could scribble down everything the women were saying.

"Would that be Malcolm Johnson?" Julia asked casually as her finger circled her cup. "I spotted his daughter, Chloe, at the meeting yesterday. She was a couple of years below me at school, but it's a small village."

Amy looked at Emily for permission to talk, but the look she received kept her silent.

"Malcolm was genetically modifying his plants with *illegal* chemicals," Emily snapped, her eyes locking with Julia's. "The results were quite beautiful, but as you can understand, it's against our rules, something you might want to tell your gran. We only allow *natural* techniques in our club."

"Understandable," Julia said with a nod. "When was he pushed out of the group?"

"Three weeks ago," Amy said quickly. "The whole group agreed he should go. It wasn't just Emily."

Emily's nostrils twitched as she continued to stare at Julia. Julia was coming to realise she knew nothing of the woman she waved to across the lane when they were both enjoying their gardens. She would never have had Emily down as the ruthless type, but her steely look of determination told Julia that she had no regrets about forcing a founding member out of the group and that she would do it again if needed.

"Aside from Malcolm, is there anyone else who would want to target your group?" Julia asked, looking at Amy once more in hopes her loose tongue would reveal even more. "Three members dead in as many weeks does suggest a pattern is emerging."

"I think you're digging in the wrong patch, Julia," Emily said with a forced laugh. "I know you have a certain *reputation* in the village for solving murders, but it's merely a coincidence that these three were members of the Green Fingers."

"*Four*," Amy said.

"Excuse me?" Emily snapped.

"Yolanda Turner," Amy mumbled with a small shrug. "She's gone too."

"Now that *was* an accident," Emily said triumphantly. "She crashed her car into a tree. If there is a pattern, which I do not think there is, she doesn't fit it."

"Yolanda was a founding member too?" Julia asked.

"She was *the* founding member," Amy said with a gulp. "It was her passion that brought us all together ten years ago. There were seven of us to start with, but the club has grown, and now half the village are Green Fingers."

Julia nodded, deciding she had extracted enough information from the women. She glanced at Emily, who stared intensely at the plate of macarons, apparently realising Julia's reason for inviting her to the café was nothing more than a ruse; a ruse that had worked.

"We should be going," Emily said, standing up and leaving her cup of tea half-finished. "I'm meeting Mary and Brendan in the pub to talk about running the club. Keep up the good work with the macarons, Julia. I'm sure they'll be perfect by the time of the party."

Emily headed for the door, leaving Amy in her seat. She stared blankly at the murky surface of her untouched tea, the weight of the world on her shoulders. She stayed there for a moment until Emily cleared her throat. She hurried after Emily, smiling apologetically over her shoulder at Julia.

Julia scribbled down everything the women had let slip, filling over three pages in her notepad. She wrote down all seven of the founding members' names on a fresh page and crossed out the four who had died in the last three weeks. She ticked off Emily and Amy's names, leaving her with the only surviving member she had not yet spoken to:

Agatha Frost

Malcolm Johnson.

***

AFTER CLOSING THE CAFÉ, JULIA DROVE to her cottage at the same time Jessie arrived home from her one day a week at college. As usual, on Wednesday evenings, Jessie had her best friends, Dolly and Dom, with her. The tall platinum blonde twins greeted Julia with a hug as always, before retreating into the cottage.

As Julia started on a simple chicken Caesar salad for dinner, Dolly and Dom sat at the counter and played on their phones and fidgeted like children, while Jessie set up the table in the garden.

"Playing anything fun?" Julia asked as she sprinkled the cooked chicken in with the romaine leaves.

"It's this new game that everyone at college is playing," Dom said without looking up. "It's just come out."

"It's so hard," Dolly added, her tongue poking out the side of her mouth.

"What's it called?" Julia asked.

"*Tetris*," Dom said, glancing up at Julia from his phone. "You've probably never heard of it."

Macarons and Mayhem

Before Julia could say anything to the contrary, Jessie came in from the garden with Mowgli in her arms and said, "I've set the table up."

Julia glanced at the cat clock on the wall with its ticking eyes and swishing tail. Their Wednesday dinner night had become her favourite event of the week, but it was not complete without Barker. He was usually there by now. She was not sure how long she could keep tossing the salad to stall them.

"He will be here soon," Julia said as she carefully sprinkled in the croutons. "He's probably just held up on a case."

"Or he is trapped in a bank, and there's a bank robber pointing a gun at him," Dom said with a thrilled smile.

"Peridale doesn't have a bank," Jessie said, flicking his ear. "I'll point a gun at you in a minute if you don't shut up."

Dom plucked a banana from the fruit bowl and pointed it at Jessie. Mowgli jumped out of her arms and scurried back into the garden.

"*Stick 'em up!*" Dom demanded. "Or I'll shoot."

Without batting an eyelid, Jessie disarmed Dom with one swift move, sending the banana flying up in the air. She caught it and pointed it at his forehead with a satisfied smile.

"Don't try it, blondie," Jessie said. "I fought scarier kids than you on the streets."

Dom let out a nervous laugh as Dolly chuckled underneath her hair. She snatched the banana from Jessie, unpeeled it and bit off the tip.

"I'm so hungry," Dolly mumbled through the mushed banana. "I could eat a family of zebras."

Julia glanced at the clock again, and then down at the salad. She passed the salad to Jessie before grabbing four bowls from the cupboard.

"It's not like it will go cold," Julia mumbled to herself as she selected cutlery from the drawer.

They walked out into the garden, where Jessie had set up the cast iron table in the middle of the grass. Tall trees surrounded her small lawn, casting a soft shadow against her cottage. Julia loved her garden. It was not prize worthy, or up to the standards of the Green Fingers, but it was her private place that felt separate from the rest of the village. It was one of the things that had attracted her to the cottage.

They ate the salad under the clear evening sky, while Dolly, Dom, and Jessie chatted about the things they had been baking during their college course. Julia tried her best to stay engaged, but her mind was firmly fixed on the recent deaths. She glanced at her watch, knowing that whatever was keeping Barker must have been serious.

When they finished eating, she took the dishes back into the kitchen, and the front door finally opened. Barker hurried in, full of apologies.

"Did I miss it?" he called as he pulled off his tie. "It's been *manic* at the station."

"It's only salad," Jessie said as she pulled his bowl from the fridge. "Anything juicy?"

"You know I can't say," Barker said, glancing at Julia to let her know he would tell her when they were alone.

They surrounded the counter in the kitchen as Barker wolfed down his salad as though he had not had a chance to eat all day. Dolly and Dom did their usual trick of asking Barker questions about his cases, wanting to know every gruesome and gory detail. He had become good at dodging their questions and speaking without revealing anything real.

When he finished, Julia poured them all glasses of the lemonade she had freshly squeezed when she had arrived home. She waited for the teenagers to naturally drift into the sitting room as they always did. Instead of following, Julia hung back.

"I had to interview Johnny again today," Barker

said quietly when the TV turned on in the other room. "I know what you're going to say, but he's the only person who seems to know what is going on."

"So, you've made him a suspect?"

"Not *officially*," Barker said defensively. "I've convinced the boss to give me more time, but he's eager to notch things up. Aside from your witness statement and the obituaries, there's no actual proof."

Julia sighed as she rubbed between her eyes. She knew it had been too good to be true when the police had eagerly lapped up her statement. When it came down to it, if things did not tick the right boxes, nothing would ever be solved.

"I've known Johnny since I was four-years-old," Julia said. "The only reason he knows so much is because he's a damn good reporter. He spotted something nobody else did. Without him, you wouldn't even have a *scrap* of evidence that any of these deaths were murders."

"He sounded quite fond of you," Barker said with a playful grin. "Spoke very highly of his old school chum."

"We went on a date once," Julia said with a shrug as she slid off the stool. "We both decided we would work better as friends."

"Both of you?" Barker asked with an arched brow.

"Yes," Julia lied. "He's a good guy. You're barking up the wrong tree there."

Barker stood up and wrapped his arms around Julia. He pulled her in, so she slipped her arms inside his suit jacket. His lips met the top of her head, soothing her in an instant.

"For what it's worth, I don't think in a month of Sundays that he did it," Barker whispered. "He's too sweet. You almost want to pet him."

"Have you got a crush on him, Barker?" Julia joked as she pulled away from the hug. "Because he *is* single."

"Very funny," Barker said with a roll of his eyes. "He has a crush on you though. Do I have to fight him? I know it will be like kicking a puppy, but he's prettier than me with those curls and doe eyes."

"You have nothing to worry about," she told him as they walked arm in arm into the sitting room. "There's only one man I love, and he's in this cottage."

"Isn't Dom a bit young for you?" Barker asked with a wink.

Julia nudged him in the ribs with her elbow before they took up the two free seats on the couch.

She looked at the TV, her head resting against Barker's shoulder. She tried to focus on the moving pictures, but her mind was somewhere else entirely.

Even though she only liked Johnny as a friend, he was a good friend, and one of only a handful of people she could say she had known and liked her whole life. If people at the station were hoping to pin the guilt on him, it only made her even more determined to discover the truth.

For tonight, however, it could wait. She sunk into Barker's side as the setting sun washed her cottage in its brilliant orange

CHAPTER 5

"I can't believe you're getting involved in *another* murder," Sue, Julia's sister, said as they walked back from The Comfy Corner after their usual weekly catch-up. "Have you ever considered that you're putting yourself in danger for *no* reason? I want my avocados to have their Auntie Julia in their lives."

Sue rubbed her growing baby bump through her

blouse. She was now sixteen weeks pregnant, and she was positively radiant, despite carrying twins. Her skin and hair were glowing in a way Julia had never seen before, and her cheeks and chest were starting to fill out to match her pert bump.

"It's not like the other times," Julia said as they headed towards Mulberry Lane. "This is Johnny's case. I'm just tagging along and doing what I can."

"You found a man's *body*!" Sue exclaimed with a strained laugh, her cheeks flushing. "Sometimes I think you're too macabre, Julia. It's not healthy."

"I don't go searching for death."

"No, but it somehow *always* finds you."

They turned onto Mulberry Lane, which was the oldest known street in Peridale. It wound like a snake, twisting and turning in an organic way. Its seventeenth century cottages had survived two world wars, storms and floods, and yet their sagging roofs and crumbling Cotswold stone exteriors were almost unchanged. Most of the cottages had been converted into small boutiques, with flats above them. Unlike the heart of the village where Julia's café was, Mulberry Lane attracted a wealthier clientele, most of whom travelled from out of the village.

After browsing Tiny Threads, a small baby clothes boutique with overpriced outfits, they headed to the antique barn at the end of the lane. Julia's stomach clenched when she saw their father talking to a customer. It had been so many years since he had worked in the barn, it felt odd to see him back in his old position. It dragged up memories of their father burying himself in his work after their mother died, which resulted in his daughters being raised by their gran. Julia pushed those memories back, remembering he was not that man anymore. Over the last few months, he had been trying his best to be part of their lives since taking over the business after his old business partner, Anthony Kennedy, had been murdered. Just knowing her father was spending more time in the village and less time cooped up in Peridale Manor settled Julia. It had been nice passing him in the street, and she still felt an almost childlike excitement when he walked unexpectedly into her café, something he had rarely done in the two years since it had opened.

"*Girls!*" he exclaimed when he spotted them. "What a lovely surprise. Here to do some shopping? I can give you a good discount. I've just had a beautiful grandfather clock come in that I think will suit your cottage, Julia."

"We're just passing," Julia said, holding out the

small bag she had been carrying. "We had dinner at The Comfy Corner, and I thought I'd drop in a slice of cheesecake."

"Katie will kill me if she finds out," he whispered with a playful wink as he accepted the bag. "But what she doesn't know won't hurt her."

"How's the baby?" Sue asked as she rubbed her own stomach.

Julia could hear the strain in Sue's voice despite her friendly smile. It had been a blow to the both of them when they had found out their father's wife, Katie, was pregnant and carrying their baby brother. Katie being the same age as Julia did not help matters either, but Sue's discovery that she was carrying twins had made her feel like she had the upper-hand over their step-mother. For the sake of the next generation, they were all trying their hardest to build bridges before the babies arrived.

"They're both doing really well," he said as he peeked into the bag. "She's eating everything in the kitchen, which is ironic because she's got me on a diet. No gluten, no sugar, no wheat, no dairy, and –"

"No fun?" Sue jumped in.

"I'm allowed a piece of fruit in the evening," he said with flared nostrils as he ran his hands through his thick hair. "I feel like a rabbit, but it's for the baby. I'm already up against it with my age, so I want to be here for as long as possible."

Julia was surprised by how selfless he was being, especially considering how little he had been in their lives. She was glad the new baby would benefit from having two parents.

Leaving their father to finish up for the day, they headed back down Mulberry Lane. They both paused when they came to the florists, Pretty Petals. A man in a wheelchair struggled to push himself through the doorway. Without needing to think about it, Julia and Sue both hurried over and held the door open for him. The man wheeled over the threshold, smiling his thanks behind obvious embarrassment.

"You never know how difficult this village is until you see it from my level," he grumbled as he ran his gloved hands over his bald head, glancing over his shoulder to the owner of the florists, Harriet, who was fiddling with the pencils in her hair, unaware of her customer's struggle. "This is why I don't go out much."

"I can't imagine it's easy getting in and out of these old buildings," Julia said as she glanced down at the bouquet of white lilies on the man's lap.

"White lilies."

"Mum's favourite," Sue whispered with a half-smile. "You have good taste."

"They're my wife's favourite," he mumbled, his eyes dropping to the flowers. "Well, they *were*."

Julia and Sue glanced at each other, both unsure of what to say. Julia opened her mouth to speak, but she couldn't find the right words. The man looked like he was only in his late-fifties. He was slender, his top-heavy frame hinting at many years spent in the chair. He had a kind, open face, but his pale green eyes were filled with sadness. Whoever he had lost, it must have been recent.

"Our mum is gone too," Sue offered. "It gets easier with time."

"Does it?" the man asked with a disbelieving laugh. "It feels like everywhere I look there's a reminder. I can't even look out of the window without seeing her in the garden. She spent most of her time there." He paused and considered his words for a moment before looking up at the two women with a kinder smile. "Thanks for your help. I'd better set off. My daughter will be wondering where I am."

With a firm grip, the man pushed himself down the winding lane until he reached Ladies Locker, one of the many boutique clothes shops. He rested outside and then waved through the window. Seconds later, a young black woman emerged, wearing a pale blue apron over her clothes. She hadn't bought anything, so her hands were free, but instead of pushing the man, she walked alongside him, talking down to him as they headed up the lane.

"I think that's Yolanda Turner's husband and daughter," Julia thought aloud, "He said he couldn't look out of the window without seeing her in the garden. He must've been talking about Yolanda's flowers."

"Poor guy," Sue said with a sigh. "Sometimes I think we were lucky with Mum. At least cancer gives you a warning and some time to prepare. Crashing your car into a tree is *so* final. I should head home. We've got the antenatal class at the village hall at six. I think Neil is keener than I am. Sitting in a circle panting and breathing with my legs spread is not my idea of a fun evening."

They reached the top of the lane, kissed each other on the cheek, and then parted ways. Julia glanced at her watch as she headed back into the village. If she hurried, she could help Jessie clear up before closing the café.

Julia rounded the corner onto the street where Edgar's cottage was. She paused to stare through the windows, her stomach turning uneasily. She had been trying not to blame herself for the poor man's death, but she could not help thinking that if she had been a little faster, she might have been able to save the man's life.

"It's a *terrible* shame," a voice cooed from behind her. "It's *no way* to go."

Julia turned quickly, unsure of where the voice had come from. She stepped forward, peering over the wall surrounding Evelyn's B&B. Julia let out a sigh of relief when she saw Evelyn sitting amongst her wild flowers. She was wearing a yellow turban with a matching kaftan, her legs crossed with the soles of her feet pointing up to the sky. Her hands rested in her lap, opening them to reveal a large crystal. She smiled up at Julia without opening her eyes.

"Did you know Edgar well?" Julia asked as she leaned against the wall.

Evelyn began to hum, and she started to rock back and forth in a circular motion. Julia wondered if the B&B owner had even heard her, or if she was too deep in her trance. Julia considered walking away to leave her to her meditation, but Evelyn sprung up suddenly like a clockwork toy. She lifted the crystal to the sky, reached up on her tiptoes and let out a groan before doubling over. She bobbed up and down before standing up normally to look Julia in the eyes with a peaceful smile.

"Hold this," Evelyn said, offering Julia the lilac crystal. "I've loaded it with the energy of the universe. It will help your guilt subside."

"How do you know I feel guilty?" Julia asked as she accepted the crystal, unsure of what to do with it.

"I saw it in the cards," Evelyn said with a knowing nod. "Feel better?"

Julia looked down at the glittering piece of rock. She waited for a sense of calm to wash over her, but nothing came.

"Maybe I'm not in tune enough for this," Julia said with a shrug as she passed it back.

"You just need to unblock your chakras," Evelyn said with another knowing nod. "I have some amazing tea inside that will help. I bought it from some monks in Tibet on one of my travels. It's not *technically* legal, but it will take you on a journey you'll *never* forget."

"I'm okay, for now," Julia said with an awkward smile, hoping Evelyn was not offended that Julia did not want any of her illegal hallucinogenic Tibetan tea. "I should get back to the café."

"You asked if I knew Edgar," Evelyn said, stepping barefoot over a patch of nettles. "I knew him as much as a neighbour would, but nothing more. I always sensed his aura was pure at the Green Fingers' meetings."

Julia suddenly remembered seeing Evelyn at the meeting. She looked around her garden, but it did not look like it had ever been tended to. It was beautiful in its own way, even if it did not possess any of the thought or refinement of the other Green Fingers' gardens she had seen. It was wild and unruly.

"Have you been a member for long?" Julia asked, eager to find out more about the dynamics of the club.

"I dip in and out when I'm not travelling," Evelyn said with a wave of her hand. "They mock my holistic approach to my garden."

"Holistic gardening?"

"I don't cut the plants," Evelyn said as though it should have been obvious. "I let them decide how they want to grow. Don't you think it's a little barbaric to trim off their leaves? How would you like it if I cut off your toes and ears because I thought you were prettier that way?"

Julia laughed awkwardly, but she immediately stopped when Evelyn did not join in. Julia straightened out her expression as she looked around Evelyn's garden once more.

"It is very pretty," she said feebly. "What you do really works."

"Thank you," Evelyn said with a wide grin as she rested her hand on her chest. "I like to think so. I spiritually guide them the best I can, but every living thing has its own destiny. Emily thinks it's a load of codswallop. She even went as far as threatening to kick me out because she didn't see the point! Yolanda *never* questioned me."

"Is Emily a tough president?"

"I think *dictator* is the right term," Evelyn said with a sigh. "It's all rather oppressive. If it wasn't for the magazine, I might have left by now. Ten thousand pounds *is* ten thousand pounds. I'm not one for material wealth, but just think of the places I could visit with that money."

"It is a lot of money," Julia agreed.

"Far too much for a prize, if you ask me," Evelyn whispered as she leaned in. "It's changing people. Somebody tossed oil over my gardenias, but I'm not surprised they were sabotaged before the judging."

"Emily did mention that she really wanted to win," Julia thought aloud. "You don't think –"

"That Emily sabotaged my garden?" Evelyn jumped in. "The cards *did* say I would be betrayed by a leader. Yes, perhaps she did."

When the conversation turned to the weather and local gossip, Julia excused herself to set off back to her café. Before she reached the door, she spotted the man in the wheelchair and the young woman heading in the direction of St. Peter's Church. They passed through the gravestones before pausing to lay down the flowers. Neither of them tried to force back their tears as they held each other.

Not wanting to stare, Julia turned to her café, her hand closing around the door handle. She cast one more look their way, but something else caught her eye. The village hall door opened and Emily and Amy slipped out. They were talking to each other, Emily's hands flapping as though she was telling Amy off for something. They headed for the exit of the church grounds, but when Emily spotted the man and young woman at the gravestone, she put her hand in front of Amy. They retreated into the shadows of the church where they waited until the young woman pushed the man out of the church grounds as he sobbed into his gloved hands. When they crept out of the shadows, they hurried back into the village hall, closing the door softly behind them.

"What are you doing?" Jessie asked through the window, making Julia jump.

"Observing," Julia replied as she hurried into the café. "There's something going on in that club, and I think it's the key to figuring out these murders."

CHAPTER 6

Leaving Jessie in charge of the café, Julia met Johnny for lunch in The Plough the next afternoon. She had not been surprised to receive a phone call from him soon after sunrise asking to meet. When she asked what he wanted to discuss, he had told her he did not want to talk about it over the phone. She had wondered if he thought her phone had been bugged, or if it was because he had somehow sensed that Barker had been lying next to her, even though he had been fast asleep.

To Julia's relief, Johnny looked like he had slept since their last meeting, even if he did not look entirely himself. As soon as they were sitting, Johnny pulled a thick pile of paperwork from his canvas bag.

"I've been digging," he said as Julia cast her eyes over the pub's lunchtime menu. "I've been collecting every scrap of information I can find on the three victims."

"And?" Julia asked, looking up hopefully. "Anything good?"

"*Nothing*!" he exclaimed. "Parking tickets, marriage certificates, tax returns, ancient out-dated qualifications, but nothing to link them, apart from being a part of the Peridale Green Fingers."

"Founding members too."

"I'd figured that part out," he said with a sigh as he sat back in his chair underneath a dreary watercolour painting of Peridale's surrounding countryside. "These people led normal, dare I say it, dull lives. The most exciting thing any of them ever did was garden. There's nothing to suggest any of them did anything offensive enough to warrant being murdered."

"Sometimes the facts say one thing, but it is not the whole picture," Julia said as she settled on fish and chips along with half a pint of Peridale Smooth lager. "For example, on paper, I'm a divorcee who runs a café, has a mortgage, and a foster daughter, but in reality, there's so much more to me than the facts."

"That is true, in your case at least," Johnny said. "On paper, I'm an English Language graduate who works at a newspaper, and in reality, I'm – *well*, I'm just an English Language graduate who works at a newspaper. There's nothing more to me, I'm afraid."

"Of course there is," Julia said reassuringly. "You're a sweet guy with a kind heart who picked up a case nobody else believed in."

"Did *you* believe me?"

Julia looked guiltily down at the menu. She was not about to lie to Johnny, but she did not know how to frame her answer without upsetting him. When she opened her mouth in hopes that something interesting would fall out, she was saved when Shelby, the feisty landlady, came over to take their orders. Johnny asked for the exact same order as Julia's; he hadn't even looked at the menu.

"*Please* tell me you have something," Johnny said as he cleaned his glasses on a napkin. "I feel like

I'm running on empty, and now that the police are sniffing around me, there's even more pressure to nail this."

"I have a plant in the club," Julia said hopefully. "I convinced my gran to join. She wasn't keen at first, but after Edgar died, I think she saw an opportunity to grasp some glory."

"Has she discovered anything yet?"

"She says they argue a lot," Julia said. "Mainly about the best types of feed for different flowers, but she says there's definitely a lot of tension in the group, and it seems to be directed at Emily."

"Their *new* president," Johnny said with a nod. "She's your neighbour. What do you know about the woman?"

"She likes her roses," Julia said. "She's nosey, but who isn't in this village? I feel ashamed to admit I've never dug any deeper. It's not that I didn't think there was anything there, I just didn't expect *this*."

"She's quite focussed," Johnny said with a nod. "I tried to talk to her, but she said she was too busy. She takes her role as president very seriously. More seriously than Yolanda did."

"Did you know much about Yolanda?" Julia asked. "She wasn't a regular in my café, so I rarely saw her."

"She was a regular in here though," Johnny said in a hushed tone, glancing at the bar. "She liked to drink. I was the one who reported about her crash, but what I didn't report was that there had been enough alcohol in her system when she died to sink a navy ship. I didn't want to embarrass her family."

"I think I met Yolanda's husband yesterday and I saw the daughter too," Julia interrupted. "Peter seemed nice, although I only spoke to him briefly."

"I found out quite a lot about her from Peter," Johnny continued. "She immigrated to the UK in the seventies from Trinidad. She worked in a factory that built circuit boards for TVs until she retired in the early nineties. You must have seen their daughter, Mercy. She's a cleaner. She is about our age now, but she didn't go to school in Peridale. Being mixed-raced back then meant she had to travel to a school where '*her kind*' would fit in. That's what Peter said, at least.

"Yolanda kept to herself until she set up the Green Fingers in 2007 with the six others. It was just something to pass the time, but it became quite popular, and she started to organise proper meetings and events for them. She seemed well liked from what I can gather, so her death must have come as a shock to them."

Macarons and Mayhem

Julia did not stop herself from pulling out her notepad while Johnny had been talking. She jotted down all the key points on a page titled '*Yolanda Turner*'. Ever since Amy had brought her up during their macaron tasting session in the café, she had been itching to learn more about Emily's predecessor.

"Do you think she's important to solving these murders?" Johnny asked after Shelby brought them their beers. "I haven't given her much thought."

"I'm not sure yet," Julia said. "It might be part of the bigger picture. If it's only the founding members that are being targeted, there might be some devil in the detail. It might not seem important, but it could be the one thing that cracks the whole case open. The more we know about all of them, the better."

A grin spread across Johnny's face as he leaned forward in his chair. He stared at Julia for a while, so much so that she turned around, wondering if there was something happening that she was not aware of.

"You're a brilliant woman," he said after a moment of silence. "Barker is a lucky man, even if he isn't the best detective inspector the force has to offer."

"He's not so bad," Julia said. "I shouldn't be

telling you this, but he convinced the men upstairs not to make you an official suspect. He knows you're only trying to help, but he needs to do his job."

Johnny appeared to think about what Julia had just said. He opened his mouth more than once to speak, but he stopped himself. When the fish and chips arrived, they ate in silence. It was not until they were finished that Julia decided to talk.

"Have you thought any more about how the obituaries turned up at the office?" Julia asked as she wiped her mouth with a paper napkin. "That's something that is puzzling me."

"We only have one camera on the front door," Johnny said with a defeated sigh. "I've checked through the footage, but I didn't see anything out of the ordinary. I've got the interns looking for every person who walked through the front door, but there's every chance we're looking for a cat burglar who climbed up the wall and through the window."

"Or they just walked through the front door?" Julia suggested. "Hiding in plain sight."

"It's crossed my mind," Johnny said, reluctantly. "I just don't understand why anyone who works at the paper would want to murder three old gardeners and go to the lengths of leaving behind clues."

Macarons and Mayhem

Julia thought about it for a moment. She slid back in her chair, replaying Johnny's words over and over in her mind until something clicked into place. She suddenly bolted up, her knees hitting the table, jostling the plates.

"It's a *fear* tactic," Julia said. "*A message.* We were *supposed* to figure out that the Peridale Green Fingers are being targeted, or else it's no fun for them. Whoever is doing this has a vendetta against certain members. They want those members to fear that they'll be next."

"But why make the deaths look like accidents?" Johnny asked with a crinkled brow. "Why not stab them, or suffocate them in their sleep?"

Julia thought for a moment, her mind playing out every scenario at lightning speed until something made sense.

"It's easy," Julia said. "It looks like an accident, but the obituaries are a message, so we know the truth, without leaving behind any obvious evidence."

"But they left behind those pink footprints," Johnny said. "What does that mean?"

"I don't know," Julia admitted. "Barker doesn't know either, or he isn't telling me."

"So, he's not telling you the finer details of the case during your pillow talk?"

"He's already been suspended once for that," Julia said, feeling herself growing defensive of Barker. "He tells me as much as he can, but he doesn't want me looking into this."

"Why are you?"

Julia thought about her reasons for a moment. She knew she craved the truth when she felt like there was injustice, but that was not the only reason this time. There was something deeper at play, and she was only just coming to realise it.

"When you asked me if I believed you, I didn't answer," Julia said softly. "I'm ashamed to say I didn't, not entirely. I trusted your judgement, but I had my doubts. When Edgar died, I realised the shoe was on the other foot for once, and I should have taken your word for it from the start."

Johnny smiled his appreciation of her admission. Julia was glad her acknowledgment of her scepticism had not upset or offended him. After they paid their bill, they walked towards the door, neither of them closer to figuring out the truth behind the Green Fingers' spike in deaths.

"What next?" Johnny asked.

"I wanted to speak to Malcolm Johnson about his dismissal from the group," Julia said. "Emily seems to think he's not capable of murder, but it's as good a motive as any."

"What's stopping you?"

"From the little I know about Malcolm, I don't think me turning up unannounced will go down well."

Johnny pulled his car keys from his pocket as they walked out of the pub. He clicked the keys, and his car beeped and flashed on the edge of the road.

"If you can take another half an hour away from your café, I have an idea," Johnny said with a twinkle in his eye.

Julia did not question him. She followed Johnny to his car, promising she would never doubt the man she had known for over thirty years again.

***

MALCOLM JOHNSON'S COTTAGE LAY down a winding dirt track on the outskirts of Peridale. It was reclusive and isolated from the rest of the village, and as Johnny and Julia drove down the lane, she came to the conclusion that it was a purposeful choice.

When they reached the cottage, the beauty of his garden took Julia's breath away. The garden was not contained by a fence, the flowers and plants looking like they had naturally sprouted from the ground with no helping hands. Green ivy covered the walls of the small cottage, with only the windows and door visible to the outside world. If it had been dark, Julia might have missed the cottage entirely.

The dirt track faded into the grass so Johnny pulled up. They walked the rest of the way. They both looked at each other as they walked towards the unknown. During their journey, Julia had told Johnny what she knew about Malcolm, none of it being particularly positive. Malcolm had a reputation for petty crime. She did not know of any crimes he had committed recently, but that did not mean the reputation had not stuck. She had heard villagers joke on more than one occasion about making sure to lock your front door in case Malcolm Johnson donned his balaclava again.

"He certainly has an eye for design," Johnny whispered as they approached his front door. "This place is amazing."

"Genetically modified, if Emily is to be believed," Julia whispered back as Johnny knocked on the door. "Although we might not want to mention that."

Julia did not like to think she was judging a man based on rumour, but even she had held her handbag closer to her body on the rare occasions she had seen him in the street. Seeing his garden and obvious talent made her feel silly for buying into local paranoia.

When the door opened, Julia let out a small gasp as she looked up at Malcolm's grand stature. She knew he was tall, but seeing him in his tiny cottage made him look like he was about to burst through the ceiling at any moment.

"*What?*" he growled. "Whatever it is, I'm not donating."

He went to close his door, but Johnny crammed his foot in the way, forcing Malcolm to open it again.

"Johnny Watson," he said with an outstretched hand. "I'm from *The Peridale Post*. This is my colleague, Julia South."

"Don't you work in the café?" he growled, his piercing eyes seeing right through Julia. "I've seen you."

Julia opened her mouth to reply, but Johnny shot her a quick look that silenced her.

"We're here to ask you some questions about the Peridale Green Fingers," Johnny said. "We're writing an exposé about the shocking way the club is run, and we thought you might have quite a lot to say, considering your unfair dismissal from the group over unfounded accusations?"

Julia gawked at Johnny, unsure if his approach was foolish or genius. From the look on Malcolm's face, he did not know what to think either.

"An exposé?" he replied with narrowed eyes. "In the paper?"

"That's right, sir," Johnny said as he pushed his glasses up his nose. "We won't take up too much of your time."

Malcolm thought about it for a moment before stepping to the side to swing the door open. Julia was too stunned to move, so she let Johnny lead the way.

Malcolm's cottage was nothing like she had expected considering his reputation. It was immaculately clean, with a light and airy feeling. The décor was tasteful, and had a definite woman's touch to it. She wondered if Malcolm's daughter, Chloe, had had a hand in the choices of patterns and colours.

He walked them through to the sitting room, which was small but not overcrowded with furniture. There was a dresser with a few framed photographs on top, a sofa and an armchair, a coffee table, and a freestanding lamp. There was no TV or any other signs of modern technology. The coffee table was completely clear, aside from a single copy of the most recent edition of *The Peridale Post*, which had been perfectly lined up with the edge of the table. Despite its already apparent perfection, Malcolm adjusted the newspaper a millimetre before sitting in the arm chair. He motioned for them to take up the sofa, which they did. Johnny reached into his canvas bag and pulled out a tape recorder before handing Julia a notepad and a pen.

"You don't mind if we record this, do you?" Johnny asked, already clicking the recorder, and placing it on top of the newspaper.

Malcolm stared wide-eyed at the tape recorder, his nails digging into the armchair. Julia could not decide if it was because it was a piece of technology, or because Johnny had tossed it on top of the newspaper so haphazardly. Malcolm nodded all the same and gulped away whatever he was feeling before turning to look Johnny dead in the eyes.

"I want whatever I say to be taken word for word," he said. "I don't want you *twisting* my words."

"That is not what we are about at *The Peridale Post*," Johnny said as he leaned on his knees. "But of course, as one of our readers, you know we're all about bringing the people honesty."

Malcolm glanced down at the newspaper again, but this time he seemed to relax a little. The way Johnny had won over the man's trust with a few well-worded sentences impressed Julia. She had never seen this side of Johnny before, but it explained how he had risen in the ranks of the newspaper over the years.

"In your own words, Mr Johnson, how would you describe the running of the Green Fingers?" Johnny asked, obviously starting off easy. "Don't think too hard about the answers. Just say what you feel."

"Do you want to know about before Yolanda died, or after?" Malcolm replied, a sneer forming on his thin lips. "Because you will get *very* different answers."

"It only feels natural to start at the beginning," Johnny said with a soft smile. "In your own time."

Malcolm thought about his response for a moment before resting his arms on his knees. His giant frame filled the chair, making it look half the size. His thinning hair was slicked neatly back, his face was well shaven, and his shirt and trousers were spotlessly clean without a single crease or piece of lint. He looked nothing like the object of fear the villagers of Peridale saw him as.

"Yolanda was the best of the best," Malcolm started, pointing a finger at Julia, who instantly started scribbling down what he was saying. "I want that noted before anything else. She was a talented gardener and a great woman. We were good friends. I never married, but I always said if I had my time again, Peter might have had a fight on his hands if I had met her back then. He knew I was joking. He's a top bloke too. He loved the bones of that woman, and rightly so. She would give you the clothes off her back if you needed them, even when people in this village weren't kind to her. A woman from Trinidad arriving in the seventies didn't sit right with a lot of people back then. It wasn't like today. Things weren't as accepted. She was up against it from the start. Nobody would give her a job, and people would say she wasn't trustworthy. It was wrong. Plain wrong. She was wasted in that factory, which was why I was the first to join her when she talked about setting up a gardening club. I even came up with the name.

"It was great in the beginning. We were all retired and getting on in life, so it gave us something to focus on. We'd go to garden centres, and meet up for social events. It wasn't always about the gardening. Yolanda made sure of that. I could tell this was her second chance at a life in this village. Times had caught up with her skin colour. People eventually realised she was just like the rest of us. There was nothing to it. If the entire village were filled with women like Yolanda, there wouldn't be a single thing to complain about. She liked a drink, but who doesn't? She wasn't addicted or anything. I wouldn't even call her a drinker, she just liked her rum. There's nothing wrong with that, is there? But people talked. Made up stories. I know what that's like. They *still* call me a *criminal!* I haven't stolen a car since 1973! Mud sticks in this village, that's why I stay out of it. If it wasn't for Yolanda, I wouldn't have left my house. She made sure I was looked after. She was my rock. Now I just have my daughter, Chloe. She's all I have now. I still have my garden, but it's not the same."

Malcolm paused for breath as Julia came to the end of her third page. She did not know shorthand, so she was trying her best to write everything word for word, even though the tape recorder was still whirring. She did not want to risk a single syllable of his statement being misinterpreted.

"And what about after Yolanda died?" Johnny asked carefully, glancing at Julia, his eyes widening when he saw how much she had written. "Did things change?"

"The poor woman wasn't even cold before Emily was prying the pin from her fingers. She went to the morgue and requested it! The silly beggars gave it to her too. Can you believe that? The group apparently held a vote, but I wasn't part of it. I would never have voted her in as the president. Yolanda always joked that if a bus hit her, I should take over. Of course, everyone knew that, which is why Emily got rid of me.

"*Genetic modification*? It was all nonsense. *Lies*! They had *no* proof. Emily started the rumour and it stuck. She mentioned my criminal past, and it scared everyone. They took another vote when I wasn't there. Got a letter in the post the next day saying I was no longer welcome in the group.

"Chloe wanted to quit on principle, but I made her stay. This garden is as much hers as mine. She's put in just as much work, and she loves the flowers. I'm surprised they haven't taken another vote to get rid of the girl considering her connection to me. Emily will do anything to hold onto power."

"Anything?" Johnny asked, edging forward.

"*Anything*!" he cried. "Margaret and Elsie were on my side. They were talking about boycotting

Emily and making me president, and then they had to go and fall down the stairs. I didn't care about it for myself, but I promised Yolanda, and that meant something to me."

"And Edgar?"

"What about him?"

"How did Edgar feel about Emily before he died?"

"Edgar is *dead*?" Malcolm asked, the shock obvious on his face as he sat back in the armchair. "Are you sure?"

"I found his body," Julia added with a sympathetic smile. "I saw somebody fleeing the scene."

"He was *murdered*?"

"Just like Margaret and Elsie," Johnny said. "They didn't fall by accident. They were pushed. Somebody has been sending warnings to the paper before the murders happened to taunt us."

Just from the look of shock on Malcolm's face, Julia knew Malcolm had nothing to do with the murders. He had been frank with them, and his reaction looked nothing but honest and true.

"So, you're saying you think Emily killed them, so her power wasn't challenged?" Johnny asked, barely able to hold the excitement in his voice.

Macarons and Mayhem

Malcolm frowned and turned to Johnny before nodding furiously.

"Yes, that is *exactly* what I am saying!" he cried. "She *must* have. She's wanted that pin since day one, and has been waiting for her chance to snatch it for herself."

Julia sighed and closed the pad. Johnny had been doing so well, but she felt like he had just put his foot right in it, and from the look on Malcolm's face, he had just given away his true intentions.

"You're not writing an exposé!" he barked, suddenly standing up. "You're just here to use me for information. Get out of my house!"

Johnny did not object. He scooped up the tape recorder and shoved it back into his bag along with the reams and reams of notes Julia had taken. They hurried to the front door before Malcom threw them out. When the door slammed behind them, Julia pinched between her brows, wondering how things could have turned so quickly.

"That could have gone better," Julia said as they set off back towards the car.

"What do you mean?" Johnny replied with a laugh. "We got *exactly* what we came for. You heard the man. He thinks Emily did it and he's just given us her motive."

"You led him," Julia said with a sigh. "You practically put the words in his mouth, and he just agreed to them."

"It's as good as!"

"It's *unreliable*," Julia snapped. "You should have just let him keep talking."

"Why does it matter?" Johnny asked, the laughter in his voice making it clear he did not understand what Julia was trying to say. "We finally have some information about how the club works."

"What if it's not the right information?" Julia replied as she ducked into the car. "If you had let him continue telling us *his* story in his *own* words, he could have told us so much more."

They sat in the car for a moment and stared at the cottage in silence, which was only broken when a car teetered down the dirt track, slowing down to a crawl as it passed them. Malcolm's daughter, Chloe, stared at them through her rolled down window, a mixture of confusion and anger written across her face. Julia could not escape her guilt for using the woman's father for information as she watched the car drive towards the cottage.

"We shouldn't have come here," Julia said. "Not like this."

"Why?" Johnny asked with another laugh.

"Because he's vulnerable," Julia snapped, unable to contain the frustration in her voice. "He's an elderly man who lives on the outskirts of our society, and you used the one thing against him that you knew would get him talking. It's not right."

"It's *journalism*," Johnny piped back as he twisted the key in the ignition. "You just don't want to admit that your neighbour could be capable of murder."

"And you don't want to admit that you've already made up your mind. You're going to use whatever story you want to fit that narrative," Julia replied as she turned to look out of the window. "I thought you were a better journalist than that, Johnny."

They drove back to the village in complete silence, the frosty atmosphere sucking the summer heat out of the car. When he pulled up outside of her café, she got out without saying a word. His wheels practically skidded on the tarmac as he sped away.

"Where have you been?" Jessie cried as she served a line of people to the door. "I need three lattes now. One soya, and the other two skinnies."

Julia did not argue. She got to work making the drinks as she thought about how she had spent her afternoon. She had heard so much information about the Green Fingers, but she did not know what to focus on. Everything appeared to point to Emily, but unlike Johnny, Julia was not going to jump to that conclusion until she had the bigger picture in front of her.

CHAPTER 7

Julia spent her Sunday morning working on her recipes for the different macarons. After a week of practice, she was happier with the results, but she still felt like they weren't quite yet up to her usual standards. She glanced at the calendar next to her fridge as she pulled another batch out of the oven, the circled date of the prize reveal only six days away.

Panicking was not going to help her, so she slid the macaron shells onto a cooling rack and leaned against her kitchen sink before picking up her notepad to scribble down the flavour adjustments. It was impossible not to flick to the notes she had made about the murders.

It had been five days since Edgar had been pushed down the stairs, and even though she had not heard from Johnny since their disagreement over their interview of Malcolm, she was sure she would have heard about another Green Finger death if one had occurred. She hoped it meant whoever was pushing elderly residents down the stairs had had a change of heart, but Julia knew they were likely biding their time and selecting which of the three surviving founding members they were targeting next.

The thought unsettled Julia. She tossed the notepad onto the counter. She started to fill the delicate macaron shells with chocolate buttercream, and tried to ignore how completely useless she felt. If it was only a matter of time until another Green Finger was murdered, all Julia could do was wait.

As she placed the final macaron on the plate, Barker's car pulled up in front of her cottage. She walked to the front door, glad to see Jessie behind the wheel. For now, the car was still in one piece.

"I think she's ready to take her test again," Barker announced as he climbed out of the passenger side of the car. "That was the smoothest lesson yet."

"Every lesson is smooth," Jessie snapped as she tossed the keys over the roof to Barker. "I'm an ace driver."

"If you ignore almost running that man over last week," Barker mumbled.

"He shouldn't have been in the road."

"It was a zebra crossing!"

"How was I supposed to notice?" Jessie replied with a roll of her eyes as she marched towards the cottage. "You told me to turn left at the end. I wasn't staring at the road, I was looking for the turning."

Jessie kicked off her black Doc Martens and jumped over the couch. She planted her feet on the coffee table, immediately burying her face in her phone. Julia knew she had lost her for the rest of the afternoon.

"Lunch at mine?" Barker suggested as he opened the boot of his car and pulled out a supermarket shopping bag. "I bought sushi and that expensive raspberry lemonade you like."

Julia closed the front door behind her and dusted the flour off her floral print summer dress. Leaving his car parked behind her vintage aqua blue Ford Anglia, they set off down the winding lane arm in arm. As they passed Emily's cottage, she bobbed up from behind her garden wall, sweat and dirt covering her red face. She pulled off her gardening gloves and rocked onto her heels.

"Nice day," Emily said as she glanced up at the sky. "Although I'd rather it wasn't so hot, but these flowers won't plant themselves."

Julia looked around Emily's garden, noticing the subtle differences. Her vast collection of well-pruned rose bushes were beautiful on their own, but bright flowers had been planted at each of their bases. There was also a new elaborate birdbath in the centre of the garden, which appeared to be made from solid marble. Between running the club meetings and schmoozing the judges, Julia was surprised Emily had squeezed in time to transform her garden.

"You've done a great job," Julia said, forcing a smile. "I'm sure the judges will love it."

"That's if they get here in time," she said as she wiped the sweat from her lined forehead. "Somebody took a pair of shears to Amy's garden and completely ruined it before she had a chance to have any photographs taken for the judging."

"Evelyn had oil thrown over her gardenias too," Julia remembered aloud. "Sounds like you have a saboteur in your ranks."

"It's not like Evelyn *ever* stood a chance of winning," Emily said with a dismissive laugh. "Holistic gardening? It's *nonsense*! But yes, it would seem that we have."

"Any idea who it could be?" Julia asked, Barker's arm tightening around hers as though to tell her to leave it. "Might be connected to the murders."

"You're not still insisting they were killed, are you?" Emily asked with an exhausted eye roll. "Honestly, Julia. I mean this with the best intentions, but maybe you should just keep your nose out for once? I know you *think* you saw someone fleeing Edgar's cottage, but it *was* an accident."

"Perhaps," Julia said through gritted teeth. "I'll leave you to enjoy the rest of your afternoon."

Barker let out a relieved sigh as they continued down the winding lane under the baking sun. They stayed completely silent until they reached Barker's cottage near the bottom of the lane.

"I'm starting to wonder if Johnny was on to

something suspecting Emily," Julia said as she unclipped Barker's gate. "The lady doth protest too much, methinks."

It appeared that Barker was holding his tongue, but the look on his face told Julia everything she needed to know. He suspected Emily too, but she knew he did not want to give her permission to get any more involved than she was. Deciding to leave it, she pulled her house keys from her pocket and selected the key Barker had given her to his cottage. Barker reached around her and opened the unlocked door.

"I finally got a cleaner," he said as he pushed the door open. "She must still be here."

Powerful disinfectant tickled Julia's nostrils as she walked into the distinctly cleaner sitting room. All of Barker's ultra-modern furniture sparkled brilliantly, the usual pizza boxes and days old cups of coffee completely gone.

"Mercy, it's just me," Barker called out as he tossed his denim jacket over the back of his white leather couch. "I thought you'd be done by now."

Julia followed him into the kitchen. The chemical fumes hit her instantly. Covering her mouth, she squinted through a cloud of steam. It cleared to reveal a woman sitting on the floor, a white mask over her mouth, goggles across her eyes, and headphones clamped over her ears. She stopped spraying the steam cleaner into the oven before ripping off her headphones, clearly startled by their arrival. When she pulled off the mask, Julia's heart skipped a beat. She was the same woman she had seen on Mulberry Lane, and later at the cemetery with the man in the wheelchair.

"I didn't hear you come in," she said with a small shaky laugh as she clicked off the old-fashioned cassette player attached to her hip. "UB40. They were always my mum's favourite."

She stood up and pulled the mask over her face. She was younger than Julia had first assumed from a distance. Just like her father, she had a kind and open face with dazzling pale green eyes, which burned beautifully against her deep skin. Julia would have guessed the woman was in her late-twenties.

"Was your mother Yolanda?" Julia asked carefully as Barker pushed open the kitchen window to let the fumes out.

"She was," Mercy said with a curt nod. "Did you know her?"

"I didn't," Julia admitted. "I run the café in the village, but I never saw her in there."

"She wasn't one for sweet things," Mercy said

with an apologetic smile. "Dad always said she had a mouth full of savoury teeth."

Mercy looked down at the cassette player attached to her belt, sadness washing over her. Julia wondered what memory she had just stumbled across.

"Do you want a cup of tea, Mercy?" Barker asked over his shoulder as he filled the kettle. "We were just about to eat lunch."

"I won't intrude." She peered into the oven before straightening up. "If you don't need to cook tonight, I can finish this tomorrow."

"He won't be," Julia answered for him. "He rarely uses the thing."

Both of the women laughed, sharing a knowing look that told Julia Mercy's father wasn't much of a cook either.

As the kettle boiled, Mercy gathered up her cleaning materials, before heading for the door. Julia raced after her, her mind whirring with all of the questions she suddenly wanted to ask the woman now she knew for certain that she was the daughter Johnny had told her about.

"Let me get that," Julia offered as she hurried around Mercy to open the door. "Need some help taking this stuff out to your car?"

Macarons and Mayhem

"I think I've got it," Mercy said, almost dropping the steam cleaner on her foot before catching it.

Julia pried the machine out of her hands and held open the front door. Mercy smiled her gratitude before they set off down the garden path towards her small Mini Cooper, which had a logo for *Peridale Cleaning Company* on the side.

"Was your mother a Green Finger?" Julia asked casually, not wanting to let Mercy know how much information she had gathered. "I think I saw her at the village hall a couple of times."

"She founded the group," Mercy said, her voice catching as she pulled her car keys from her pocket. "Not that they thanked her for it in the end. You'd never even know what my mother did for them now Emily is in charge."

Julia picked up on the venom in the woman's voice. She began to wonder if any members of the club actually liked Emily. She considered Amy for a second, but the poor woman seemed more scared of her than anything.

"I heard she's been quite a force since taking over," Julia said as she placed the steam cleaner into the boot of the small car. "I heard that Malcolm was the natural fit to take over."

"He *should* have taken over, but he's not a forceful man, despite what people think." Mercy carefully placed her cleaning products next to the steam cleaner. "Some cold-hearted journalists went to his cottage to pry information out of him. Poor guy barely leaves his house, and he's still getting harassed in his own home."

Julia gulped down her guilt, hoping it did not register on her face. Mercy shut the boot, so Julia stepped back onto the pavement.

"Thanks for your help," Mercy said. "I'll see you around."

"Yeah, I suppose you will," Julia said, glancing over her shoulder at Barker's cottage. "Can I ask you one more thing?"

Mercy closed her fist around her keys before nodding. Julia looked up the lane to Emily's cottage, where her head was bobbing up and down amongst the roses. She was probably still on her hands and knees furiously stuffing as many flowers into the soil as her poor garden could handle.

"You mentioned that people wouldn't know what your mother had done for the group now that Emily was in charge." Julia paused and folded her arms against her chest. "What do you really think of Emily? She's my neighbour, but I've seen a different side of her recently."

"Honestly?" Mercy asked, her defined brows arching a little. "She's a snake. I never got too involved with my mum's club. Gardening wasn't my thing, but I still heard things. Mum hated Emily. She said she took the club too seriously and had itchy feet to lead. It was supposed to be a fun project for retired people. Emily always took it too far. Mum said that when she was applying to the magazine to get featured, all Emily talked about was the prize. I don't even think she's bothered about the money, she just wants the title of having the best garden in Peridale."

Julia stepped back into Barker's garden. She thanked Mercy for talking to her and watched as she drove carefully down the lane and into the village.

"She's a nice girl," Barker said as he put the plates of Sushi on the dining room table. "Good cleaner too. I thought I was quite tidy until she came in."

"You were never tidy, Barker," Julia said as she took a seat at the table. "I feel for her. She's lost her mother, and now Emily is parading around with that badge on acting like she's always been in charge."

"It's just a silly little club." Barker filled her glass with raspberry lemonade. "You can't keep thinking about it. We're working on it. We've got some leads."

"I suppose you're not going to tell me?" Julia asked, leaning into Barker's side. "Because if you do, it won't leave my lips."

"You're right," Barker said with a wink. "I'm not going to tell you, especially since you're such good friends with one of our suspects."

"If you're talking about Johnny, I don't think he'll be talking to me anytime soon. We spoke to Malcolm about the club. Johnny told him he was writing an exposé. The poor guy believed him. I thought it was a clever tactic until Johnny started putting words into Malcolm's mouth."

"I heard about that." Barker sucked the air through his teeth. "I hoped Malcolm had been wrong about '*the café lady*'."

"I feel awful," Julia said. "I knew he was a recluse, but I didn't think Johnny would manipulate him like that."

"You're not an angel either, Julia," Barker replied with a soft smile. "Maybe you just don't like seeing yourself in other people."

Julia opened her mouth to object, but she immediately stopped herself. How could she protest when she knew Barker was right? She suddenly felt like a fool for getting on her high horse when she had carried out similar techniques when she had been trying to discover information.

"I think I owe Johnny an apology," Julia whispered, almost to herself as she stared off into the corner of the room. "Is that a typewriter?"

Julia stared at a clunky typewriter on top of a mahogany desk, neither of which she had ever seen before. Considering how much they stuck out amongst the white wood and glass, she was surprised she had not spotted them right away.

"I bought them from your dad's barn," Barker said quickly, his cheeks blushing.

"A typewriter?" she asked again, arching a brow. "What are you going to do with that?"

"Tap dance." Barker strained a laugh as he crammed a piece of sushi into his mouth. "What else am I going to do with it? Write, of course."

"Write what?"

"Nothing," he replied, his cheeks burning even more. "Try the sushi. It's really tasty."

Julia picked up the small chopsticks and a piece of the sushi with it. She dunked it in the dish of soy sauce, lifting it to her mouth, but she stopped before it reached her lips.

"It wouldn't have anything to do with what I

saw in your briefcase?" Julia asked carefully as she watched Barker cram more sushi into his mouth.

"I told you that was nothing too," Barker mumbled through the rice and seaweed.

"So, you're writing *nothing* on a typewriter, and you have *nothing* typed up in your briefcase?" Julia replied with a smirk. "It doesn't take a detective inspector to connect the dots, Detective Inspector."

Julia tossed the sushi into her mouth and chewed in silence, satisfied with her response. Barker tugged at his shirt collar, avoiding the typewriter in the corner of the room as though it was swelling and growing to fill the entire cottage.

"I'll tell you soon," Barker said after sipping his raspberry lemonade and glancing uncomfortably. "Can we just enjoy the sushi for now?"

"Okay, Barker. I won't bring it up again," Julia said as she dipped another roll into the soy sauce. "I promise."

"And you won't go trying to break into my briefcase again?"

"I promise."

"Are your fingers crossed under the table?" Barker asked, arching a brow.

"No." Julia quickly uncrossed her fingers resting in her lap. "You're right. This is good sushi."

Macarons and Mayhem

They ate the rest of the sushi in peace and chattered idly about their weeks at work, both of them avoiding the Green Fingers case. When they were finished, they cleared away the dishes and wandered back up to Julia's cottage. Julia glanced through the sitting room window as she walked down the garden path. When she saw Jessie and Billy kissing on the couch, she put her hand up and stopped Barker. She watched with a grin for a second before turning Barker around to head back to the road.

"Let them be teenagers," Julia whispered as she carefully closed the garden gate. "She still thinks we don't know they're together."

"You know they're not the only ones who can be teenagers," Barker said before cupping Julia's cheek and kissing her. "C'mon, let's go for a drive. The afternoon is still young."

CHAPTER 8

Julia and Dot walked to the village hall for another Green Fingers meeting, each of them carrying half a dozen boxes of macarons.

"I'm just not cut out for this club, Julia," Dot whispered as they walked across the church grounds. "My hands are as dry as sandpaper, and I've spent so much time bent over in my garden I don't think my spine will ever be the same."

Macarons and Mayhem

"I thought you might hear something useful, but maybe it's not worth it," Julia said, her chin resting on the boxes. "Whatever is going on with this club, I doubt they're going to discuss it with everyone."

"There's not much discussion at the moment," Dot said as she pulled on the village hall door. "I don't know if this is how it always is, or if this is just how Emily runs things, but most meetings devolve into arguments. They're not even arguing about flowers either. It's usually Emily who starts them. I'm sure every time she senses her authority is being challenged, she snaps."

They walked into the village hall, and the complete silence stunned Julia. The excitement of her first experience of the group was gone. She looked into the sea of faces standing around the room, none of them talking. She looked past them to Emily and Amy, who were whispering with Mary and Brendan from the magazine, but the reporters looked like they were trying to get away.

"I brought macarons," Julia announced, hoping to relieve the tension. "I thought we could have a tasting before the party."

To Julia's relief, a small murmur of excitement rippled through the group, but it did not last long. Emily marched through the crowd, pushing people out of the way, her pin shining proudly.

"*Julia!*" Emily cried with a manic smile, her eyes bulging out of her head. "What are you doing here? You're *not* a member."

"No, but I am," Dot said as she dragged Julia over to the tables at the side of the room. "We've brought some macarons for your *royal highness* to approve."

"I would have preferred if you had called ahead," Emily said, her tense smile widening so much it looked like it might crack her face in two. "We're a little busy."

"Be *quiet*, Emily!" Evelyn cried as she pushed the president aside, her bright pink kaftan fluttering behind her. "You heard the woman. She's brought us macarons to taste, so let's taste them!"

The group mumbled their agreement as they walked around Emily towards the table. Julia stood back to watch them open the boxes. She was pleased to hear them commenting on the pretty colours and fragrances.

"Macaron?" Dot said as she walked across the room to present a macaron to Emily. "They are quite delightful."

Emily slapped the macaron out of Dot's hand, sending it flying across the room. A gasp shuddered through the crowd as Dot clutched her hand to her chest. The president stared down at Dot, her figure growing with each frenzied pant. She glanced around the room, her eyelids flickering as she made eye contact with her members.

"This is a *closed* meeting," Emily cried, her bottom lip wobbling out of control as she looked back at Dot. "I – *I need to go*."

Emily turned on her squeaky heels and walked quickly to the door, each footstep echoing around the hall as though it was empty. When the village hall door slammed, the chatter erupted. Julia hurried over to her gran's side.

"Are you okay?" she asked, looking down at Dot's hand.

"The little *witch*!" Dot cried, turning to the door. "She's lucky she caught me by surprise, or I might have hit her so hard that she and that precious pin ceased to exist!"

Mary and Brendan stepped forward, the shock clear on their faces. They tiptoed around the group as though expecting one of the villagers to strike out and attack them too. Julia wanted to tell them it wasn't a regular occurrence, but she could not find the words. The truth was, she had no way of explaining Emily's behaviour.

"This village is *something*," Mary whispered to Brendan as she scribbled furiously on her clipboard. "I have no idea what the editor was thinking sending us here."

"Mental," Brendan mumbled as he crouched down to take pictures of the spoiled macaron. "Absolutely *mental*."

Julia turned her attention back to the members. They chatted freely as they enjoyed the French treats, the sudden disappearance of their leader seeming to ease them. Julia took a step back, wondering if she should leave them to it. She stopped herself when she spotted one woman sitting on the edge of the room staring intensely at her. It was Malcolm's daughter, Chloe, and she was the only one who had not dived in to grab a macaron. Julia turned back to the door, but she gulped down her pride, knowing she owed the woman an explanation.

"Hi," Julia said as she approached her carefully. "Not hungry?"

"I don't want anything from *you*, thank you," Chloe said with a snide smile as she crossed one leg over the other, her sharp blonde bob dancing around her face. "Not after what you did to my father."

"I wanted to apologise about —"

"What good are your apologies?" Chloe snapped, suddenly jumping up, so she was nose to nose with Julia. "He was up all night cleaning the cottage. He's not well."

"I never knew."

"You wouldn't! People don't ask!" Chloe cried, tossing her arms out. "You all just assume he's still that criminal he was when he was a kid. Decades have passed, but Peridale never forgets. The only person who cared was Yolanda, and she's – *she's gone*."

Chloe took a step back and looked down at the floor. Julia's instinct told her to hug Chloe, but her brain vetoed the idea.

"I really *am* sorry," Julia whispered softly as she joined Chloe in looking down. "We just wanted to figure out what was happening, so it didn't happen to anyone else. If there's anything I can do, just –"

"There *is* something you can do," Chloe said, looking up into Julia's eyes. "*Leave him alone*."

Chloe's shoulder slammed into Julia's as she pushed past her. Julia glanced to the empty macaron boxes, wondering why she thought it had been a good idea to come to the meeting. Leaving her gran behind, she headed for the door before she caused more trouble.

She pulled on the door, jumping back as Peter wheeled himself in, his face bright red, and his eyes piercing. He either did not recognise Julia as the woman who had helped him out of the florists, or he did not see her.

"*You!*" he cried as he wheeled himself towards Mary and Brendan. "You sly little –"

"*Whoa,* wheels!" Brendan cried out as he jumped in front of Mary with his arms spread out. "Calm down, yeah?"

"*Calm down?*" Peter cried, his voice shrill. "How can I calm down when I've just heard that you're not going to include any mention of my Yolanda in the magazine? I just ran into Emily. She was more than happy to fill me in!"

Silence descended on the village hall again, all eyes turning to stare at the furious wheelchair bound widower. Mary and Brendan stared at each other, neither of them appearing to know how to respond.

"It won't fit with our readers," Mary said with an excusing laugh. "We're not a tabloid rag! We're a serious magazine. We can't just start writing about drunk women crashing their cars!"

There was a split second of calm before Peter launched his chair forward with one swift push of his arms. Dot dove forward and grabbed the handles to pull him back, but not before his fingers closed around Brendan's shirt.

"*Some drunk women?*" Peter screamed. "*How dare you*! That was my *wife*! This was *her* group! You're only here because of *her*! She spent *years* trying to convince your *stupid* magazine to come here!"

"I beg your *pardon*!" Mary cried. "How dare *you*, you pathetic little –"

Brendan glanced over his shoulder at Mary and gave her a look that instantly shut her up. Peter tried to wheel forward again, but Dot pulled on his chair with all of her strength.

"*Alright*!" Peter cried, pushing Dot's hands off his chair. "I'm going. You're all cowards. Yolanda is turning in her grave right now at what has become of her group."

All eyes suddenly darted to the floor as Peter wheeled himself to the door. Julia walked forward to hold it open for him, but he burst through and disappeared.

"I've had *quite* enough of this village!" Mary called. "C'mon, Brendan. Let's go back to the hotel."

Mary stormed out of the room, followed by Brendan, who snapped more than one shot of the shocked members' faces as he left.

"See what I mean?" Dot cried to Julia as she shuffled past her. "Are there any macarons left because I'm – *oh*, you greedy bunch! There's not even a single crumb."

Julia pinched between her eyes. She was so exhausted with the Peridale Green Fingers; she almost did not want to bake for the prize reveal, whether she was being paid or not.

"Julia?" a soft voice called after her as she walked through the church grounds.

Julia turned to see Amy slipping out of the village hall. Her roller-set hair looked out of place, and she looked like she had not been sleeping recently. Instead of her usual hues of pale pink and blue, she was wearing a grey cardigan and a black skirt. She did not look anything like the woman Julia knew.

"Please don't judge Emily too hard," she whispered as she glanced back at the village hall. "She's a little stressed at the moment. Mary just broke the news that Emily wouldn't be eligible to win the prize because she was the president of the club. They told Yolanda, but she never passed on that message. That was Yolanda though. She didn't need somebody to tell her she had the best garden because she knew she did, and that was without being arrogant about it."

"Isn't that ironic?" Julia replied softly. "Emily wanted to be president so badly, but it's ended up being a double-edged sword."

"She's worked *hard* on her garden," Amy said, the defence loud in her voice. "She *deserved* it."

"Haven't you *all* worked hard on your gardens?"

"Well, yes, but Emily cares more," Amy whispered. "It's not like I'm eligible to win now anyway. Somebody destroyed my garden before it was officially judged."

"Somebody must have *really* wanted to win to do that," Julia said firmly as she looked Amy straight in the eyes.

"You don't think –"

"That Emily destroyed your garden to better her own chances?" Julia replied with a sigh. "I don't know my neighbour like I thought I did. I wouldn't have said she would have slapped a macaron out of my gran's hands, but we all saw what she did."

Amy thought about what Julia had said for a moment before letting her fingers drift up to her lips. She shook her head for a brief second before narrowing her eyes and staring hard at Julia.

"I don't like to think she would," Amy said, the

wobble in her voice betraying her. "But she has been acting *differently* as of late."

"In my experience, you never really know a person until they show you what they're capable of," Julia said as she rested a hand on Amy's shoulder. "I need to get back to my café, but you're welcome to come with me for a cup of tea and a slice of cake on the house. I didn't see you get a macaron."

Amy did not object. She let Julia lead her around the village green and into her café. After she put the tea and cake in front of her, Amy seemed to relax, but every time the café door opened, they both jumped as though expecting Emily.

Emily did not show her face for the rest of the afternoon, but she did not leave Julia's mind. Had Johnny been right about her own connection to Emily blinding her judgement? Like Amy, she did not want to think her neighbour could be capable of such horrid things, but the more she thought about it, the more Julia disliked the conclusions she was coming to.

CHAPTER 9

The café was quiet the next day, so Julia poured her heart and soul into baking the most important cake she had made in a long time. She measured every ingredient impeccably, watched it bake so she knew when it was finished, and spent hours decorating its exterior, not stopping until it was nothing less than perfect.

After sending Jessie up to the cottage after

closing the café, Julia fastened the cake into the passenger seat of her aqua blue Ford Anglia. She kept one eye on the cake at all times as she drove through the village, especially when she rattled down the bumpy dirt track to Malcolm's cottage.

Julia pulled up behind two cars, one of which she recognised as Chloe's. She sat for a moment and stared at the beautiful garden. Was she making the right decision? Even though Chloe had told her to stay away, she could not ignore how she had left things with Malcolm. She unbuckled the cake, hoping the faith she had in her baking to heal wounds was not unfounded.

With the cake box in hand, she crept towards the cottage. She had already decided that if she were not invited inside, she would leave the cake on the doorstep in hopes they found it before the rats.

Gulping down her fear, Julia walked up to the door. Voices drifted from the sitting room, but she could not see through the shadowy curtains. Knowing it was now or never, she pressed the doorbell, stepped back, and waited.

Julia did not know if she was relieved or scared when it was Chloe who answered the door. She did not immediately slam the door in Julia's face like she had feared, but she did not look pleased to see her.

"You have *some* nerve," Chloe said as she folded her arms, her sharp blonde bob wiggling as she moved her head. "I thought I told you to stay away."

"I know," Julia said quickly, her voice shaking. "I just wanted to give your father this. I baked it especially."

Julia opened the cake box to show Chloe her creation. Chloe peered into the box, her brows twitching sceptically. Behind the anger, Julia could tell she was impressed.

"You made this?"

"It's sort of what I do," Julia said with a small shrug. "You can give it to him. Just tell him that I'm sorry. I really am sorry, Chloe."

Chloe looked down at the cake again before stepping to the side. Julia almost could not believe her luck, but she was not about to turn down the invitation.

"Can you take your shoes off?" Chloe asked as she closed the door behind her. "It usually doesn't bother him, but he's in a bad way."

Julia complied and carefully kicked off her shoes, placing them next to the door. She let out a small gasp when she stepped onto the wet floorboards. The scent of bleach was almost overpowering.

Chloe led Julia into the sitting room, and she was surprised to see that Malcolm was not alone. Peter sat in his wheelchair in between the couch and the sofa. They both turned to look at the new arrival, both of them giving her similar confused looks.

"You've got another visitor, Dad," Chloe announced loudly. "This is your lucky day."

Malcolm bolted up in his chair before quickly running his fingers through his slicked back thin hair. He glared at Julia like she was a bomb that was about to explode. She pushed forward her friendliest smile, but it did not seem to make a difference.

"I know you," Peter said, pointing a finger at Julia. "You're the woman who helped me out of the florist last week."

"She runs that café in the village," Chloe explained as she hovered behind the couch. "She *doesn't* work at the newspaper."

Julia wanted to explain that it had been Johnny who had said she worked at the newspaper, but she knew it was probably a good idea not to mention him.

"I brought you something." Julia took a step forward, her toes squelching on the soaking carpet. "I hope you like angel food cake."

Macarons and Mayhem

"It's his favourite," Chloe said, arching a brow suspiciously. "How did you know?"

"Lucky guess." Julia did not want to admit she had asked every person who came into her café until somebody answered. "Can I show you?"

Malcolm looked at Chloe, who gave him an encouraging nod, which relaxed him a little. Malcolm stood up and picked up the lone newspaper that was still perfectly aligned on the coffee table. He pulled off the outside sheet and set it on the couch before motioning for Julia to sit. She did not question him. Peter smiled apologetically at her as though to let her know this was typical behaviour.

Julia eased herself onto the newspaper, making sure not to touch anything. The last thing she wanted to do was upset Malcolm more. She pulled off the lid and presented the cake to him, the paper crinkling under her behind.

"*Wow*! Look at that, Malcolm!" Peter exclaimed. "It's your garden!"

Malcolm looked down at the carefully crafted flowers Julia had created. Just like Malcolm's garden, they covered every inch of the cake, their colours and shapes representing the flowers in his well-designed patch of land. Julia had created it from memory, but she thought she had done a good job at reconstructing it.

"Is that the jasmine?" Malcolm asked, pointing a brave finger at a patch of white flowers on the left side of the cake.

"That's what I was going for."

"It's perfect," he said, a small smile flickering across his lips. "You made this for me?"

Julia nodded, warmth spreading through her chest. Just from the openness of his old face, she knew the cake had done the trick.

"It's an apology," Julia said carefully as she passed the cake to him. "We should never have come here and lied to you. It was wrong of us, but we had good intentions."

Malcolm accepted the cake and stared down at the design, his eyes drifting over the dozen different details Julia had spent hours crafting. Most people did not see the point in spending so long on something that was going to be eaten, but Julia did. The look on Malcolm's face made every second worth it.

"Get some plates," Malcolm called to Chloe. "It almost seems too beautiful to cut, but I want to see if it tastes as good as it looks."

Julia took the cake back before following Chloe

into the kitchen, which was as immaculate as the rest of the cottage. The work surfaces were completely clear, making the ones in her cottage look cluttered. The scent of bleach hit her again.

"That's the first time I've seen him smile all week," Chloe said as she pulled four plates from the cupboard. "Who knew all it would take was a cake? Would you do the honours?"

Chloe handed Julia a large plate and a dazzling knife. Julia carefully pulled the cake out of the box and transferred it to the plate. She cut four generous slices.

"Crumbs," Chloe whispered as she quickly dusted the cake remnants into her hands before throwing them in the shining stainless steel bin. "It's better that he doesn't see them."

"I really am sorry," Julia said as Chloe pulled four forks from a sparse cutlery drawer. "Not just for lying to your father, but for everything."

"Everything?"

"He lives on the fringes of the village, and I've never once thought to come and visit him."

"You can't apologise for the whole village," Chloe mumbled as she placed the forks on the plates. "I sometimes wonder how different things would have been if we didn't live in this village. He might have had a second chance. I'm just glad he had Yolanda. She saw through the gossip and got to know him."

"It's not too late for him."

"Really?" Chloe replied with a sarcastic laugh. "I can't see the whole village changing their minds about him anytime soon. He had the Green Fingers, but he doesn't even have that anymore."

Julia followed Chloe through to the sitting room with the cake. She was surprised to see the newspaper no longer on the couch. They tucked into the cake, which was as delicious as Julia could have hoped for.

"I heard the café was good, but I never knew it was *this* good," Peter exclaimed after licking his fork. "Ever thought about putting in a ramp for disabled access?"

"I can do," Julia said. "Although I'm ashamed to say it has never crossed my mind before."

"Don't worry, it didn't cross mine before I was stuck in this thing," he said, tapping a finger on a faint scar on the side of his head that Julia had not noticed before. "That pesky tumour made sure I didn't forget it anytime soon. This chair was easier when I had Yolanda but – *but I* can't really put this burden on Mercy."

"I'm sure she doesn't mind," Chloe said as she put her plate on the table.

"She's a good girl." Peter looked like he was holding back tears. "But she deserves better than being lumped with me and this chair. She doesn't drink, or smoke, or take drugs, and she's a hard worker. I couldn't ask for a better daughter."

"Spitting image of Yolanda too," Malcolm said with a sigh. "She's a smashing girl."

Peter slapped his hand on top of Malcolm's, and the two men shared the same sad smile. Julia almost felt sad that she had not known Yolanda. The void she had left in these men's lives showed how much of an amazing woman she was.

As though not wanting to linger in the silence, Peter unlocked the brakes on his chair and wheeled himself back.

"I'll be back to see you soon," Peter said as Malcolm stood up. "We need to stick together in this village. You look after him, Chloe."

"I always do," she replied curtly. "I'll show you out to your car."

Chloe followed Peter out of the living room, leaving Malcolm and Julia alone. Her instinct told her to apologise again, but it did not seem like it was needed. Instead, she stood up, deciding she was not going to impose on the man any longer.

"You're always welcome in my café," Julia said as she walked to the door. "Anytime you want."

"Thank you," he said as he stood up again, his giant frame filling the small cottage. "You might just see me in there."

Julia smiled at the man one last time before walking along the damp floorboards to the front door. She pushed her soggy toes back into her shoes and then opened the front door. She turned back before she closed it, seeing Malcolm in the kitchen pouring a bottle of bleach into a mop bucket. Julia hoped he would accept her invitation to her café. She knew Peridale could be an awful place to be if you were on the wrong side of the gossip, but Julia had found that the villagers were more forgiving than they appeared. People needed to get to know the real Malcolm to see he was not a criminal to be feared, but just a gentle giant.

Julia walked towards her car as Peter pulled himself into his driver's seat with special handles in the ceiling. Chloe collapsed and loaded his wheelchair into the boot.

"Don't be a stranger," Chloe said as she shut Peter's car door. "He loves it when you visit."

"It's been a rough month, but things are starting

to look up," Peter said after winding the window down. "I can see why Yolanda was so fond of him."

Chloe waved one last time before he drove off, leaving the women alone.

"I'll see you around, Julia," Chloe said with a kinder look than the one she had given Julia when she first arrived at the cottage. "Thanks for proving me wrong. You're not a bad person."

Chloe walked back to the cottage, showing a glimpse of Malcolm mopping the hallway floor before she closed the door. Julia pulled her keys from her pocket. Things had gone better than she could have hoped for, making her glad she had listened to her instincts to make things right.

She walked towards her car, glancing back at the beautiful cottage once more. It was a shame that Malcolm was not part of the Green Fingers anymore because as far as Julia was concerned, he had the most beautiful garden in Peridale. Considering how the last meeting had turned out, maybe Emily dismissing him had been a blessing in disguise.

She turned back to her car, but something sparkled under the sunlight in the backseat of Chloe's car. Julia peered through the window, her heart stopping when she saw a can of engine oil poking out from under a blanket. It wouldn't have been such an unusual thing to find in the backseat of a car if a pair of gardening shears had not accompanied it.

Julia thought about Evelyn's oiled gardenias and Amy's destroyed garden. Turning back to the cottage, she thought about Chloe's parting words. Chloe might have thought Julia was a good woman, but Julia was not sure she could return the compliment. Cupping her hands against the glass, her heart stopped when she saw a blood red rose petal stuck in between the blades of the shears.

***

JULIA DROVE AS QUICKLY AS SHE DARED through the village, not stopping until she saw Johnny walking away from her café. She pulled up beside him and threw open the passenger door.

"I've got another one," Johnny called as he got into her car. "It's –"

"Emily?" Julia answered for him.

"How did you know?"

"Lucky guess," she replied. "I'm sorry about calling you a typical journalist. I was a hypocrite."

"It doesn't matter," Johnny said as he yanked the seatbelt across his chest. "We need to get up to

Emily's cottage. I've been out of the office all day. I don't know how long this was sitting on Rhonda's desk. I've already called the police."

Julia sped up to Emily's cottage, taking the bends sharper than ever before. Johnny did not tell her to slow down. She pulled up outside of the cottage, spotting the destroyed roses in an instant. Her heart sank to the pit of her stomach; they were too late.

They jumped out of the car at the same time a police car sped down at them from the opposite direction. Two uniformed officers jumped out, one of them mumbling into his radio.

"I called you," Johnny cried as he unclipped Emily's garden gate. "I got another obituary."

Johnny stepped to the side to let the officers walk down the garden path. They gave each other sceptical looks, and just from the way they stared at Johnny told Julia they still suspected him.

Instead of lingering back, Julia stepped into the garden, the destroyed ruby rose petals crunching underfoot. Years of Emily's effort had been destroyed in seconds. Julia no longer cared about the things Emily had done, she did not deserve this.

"*Mrs Burns?*" one of the officers called into the house as he banged a fist on the door. "It's the police. Can you come to the door?"

A faint groan drifted from within the cottage, breaking the silence. The officers looked at each other, and then to Julia and Johnny.

"*Mrs Burns?*" one of the officers called out again. "Are you –"

"*Get out of the way!*" Julia cried. "*She's in there!*"

Without a second thought, Julia thrust herself at the cottage door, and unlike Edgar's, this one burst open. She clasped her arm as it began to throb, but she quickly forgot the pain when she saw Emily lying in a puddle of blood on the kitchen floor. The old woman let out another groan as her eyelids fluttered.

"We need an ambulance," one of the officers mumbled into his radio with a shaky voice. "*Quickly.*"

Julia pushed past them and arrived at Emily's side. There was nothing she could do to change the situation so she clutched Emily's hand and squeezed.

Julia looked down at the ground with a heavy heart. Her eyes opened wide when she landed on a faint pink boot print on the pale tiles, just like the ones she had found in Edgar's kitchen.

"It's going to be okay," she said as she listened out for the sirens. "You're going to be okay."

CHAPTER 10

"We need to go to the police with this," Johnny whispered to Julia as they hurried across the church grounds. "If Chloe killed Emily, we need to stop her before she does it again."

"We don't know that she killed anyone," Julia whispered back.

"The oil and the shears suggest she did."

Julia thought back to what she had seen in the back of Chloe's car, but she was not so sure anymore. The more she thought about it, the less strange it felt for a member of the Green Fingers to have a pair of gardening shears in the backseat of the car.

"I was with Chloe when Emily was hit," Julia whispered as she pulled on the door of the village hall.

"Emily could have been there for hours. I went to the hospital this morning, and they said she'd lost a lot of blood."

"Did you see her?"

"They wouldn't let me in," he said solemnly. "I don't think it would have made much difference. She wouldn't have been able to hear my apology anyway. She's still unconscious."

They walked into the meeting, the sombre mood hitting Julia. Amy, Mary, and Brendan were sat at the front, looking out at the group like teachers in a school assembly. Some of the members dabbed their eyes with tissues, but most of them looked too stunned to shed any tears.

"You're here," Amy called with a nervous smile, standing up from her seat. "Please, come to the front."

Macarons and Mayhem

Julia and Johnny looked uneasily at each other as they walked around the crowd of people who were all looking expectantly at them. Julia had been surprised when Amy called first thing that morning to ask her to come to the meeting.

"I should have *warned* Emily," Evelyn said heavily as she adjusted her lemon yellow turban. "I could *feel* something *dark* was coming for her."

"Give it a *rest*, Evelyn," Amy snapped, her raw eyes narrowing to slits. "She might not – she *might* not recover. Now isn't the time to advertise yourself."

Amy was dressed head to toe in black, devoid of her usual pastel shades. The only colour on her outfit came from the presidential green pin on her breast pocket. It jumped out at Julia, flashing like a beacon.

"Why did you call me here?" Julia asked, looking at Mary and Brendan who looked just as confused as she felt. "Do you have any news about Emily?"

"No," Amy sniffled as she dabbed her nose with a black handkerchief. "I visited her this morning. She's in intensive care. *Oh, Julia!* You should have seen her. All those tubes – she looked like a monster!"

Amy sobbed wildly into her hands, an eerie silence filling the vast hall. Mary reached out to comfort her, but stopped herself before her hand made contact with Amy's shoulder. The judge rested her hands in her lap, and then looked at Brendan who could only offer a shrug. He pulled his camera up to take a picture of Amy, but Mary shook her head disapprovingly.

"I'm sorry," Amy said as she dried her eyes. "I'm still in shock. I think I need a sweet tea and a nap, but there's no time for that."

"Why are we here, Amy?" Julia repeated, already starting to feel a little frustrated.

"Yes," Amy said, suddenly standing up and offering her chair to Julia. "I need you to tell us everything you know about this killer. Two murders might have been excusable, maybe even three, but now that Emily's life is hanging in the balance, we're all terrified that it's going to be one of us next."

The scared faces stared desperately at Julia as though she was their new leader. Julia opened her mouth to speak, but looked hopelessly at Johnny, and then Amy. She did not know where to start.

"It's not *all* of you that are being targeted," Johnny said, stepping forward to the front of the group. "It seems that *only* the founding members are being targeted."

There was a collective sigh of relief from everyone except Amy. She gasped, her hand resting against her mouth. She looked at Julia for reassurance, but Julia could not give it. With only two founding members alive and well, Amy's odds of surviving had been slashed.

"What do we do?" Shilpa Patil, the post office owner, called out. "We can't just stand by and let this happen again! What are the police doing about it?"

"Not a lot," Johnny said. "Not that I can see, anyway."

After Emily had been taken away in an ambulance, Julia and Johnny had gone to Julia's cottage and properly cleared the air. Johnny promised he was not going to jump to conclusions again after focussing too hard on Emily. As the chatter in the room started again, Julia could not help but feel Johnny was jumping harder than ever before.

"They're doing *everything* they can," Julia called out, standing up to join Johnny. "The truth is, there isn't much evidence. Whoever is doing this is moving unseen. They're clever and calculated. This has been planned out. From planting the obituaries in the newspaper office, to gaining entry to the victims' houses, they know exactly what they're doing."

"I thought the others were pushed down the stairs?" Brendan called out as he took a picture of the group. "I heard Emily had her skull bashed in."

"Emily doesn't *have* stairs," Amy said, throwing a strong look in the photographer's direction.

"I think the killer is getting desperate," Julia suggested. "Time is running out for them. With each new death, it's going to be easier to track them down."

"But it *must* be someone we all know," Shilpa cried as she clutched her sari. "It could be someone in this room!"

They all turned to face each other, their eyes filled with suspicion.

"It *is* a possibility," Johnny agreed as he adjusted his glasses. "Which is why we need to talk about it. Some of you must know something, even if you don't realise it. Who would want to target you?"

"*Malcolm!*" one of the women cried. "*He's* the criminal!"

"What about that man from the garden centre?" a man shouted out. "We broke that water feature on our last visit."

Johnny began to scribble down their suggestions as they all aired their grievances one by one, but Julia did not bother. She knew for somebody to commit several murders they needed to have a strong motive. Julia turned to Amy, sure she was keeping a secret. Amy stared blankly into the distance, unblinking and still. If Amy was hiding something, Julia had no idea how she was going to unlock it.

"*I* have an idea," a voice called from across the village hall. "And *she's* standing *right there*."

All heads turned to face Chloe as she let the doors shut behind her. She walked into the hall, her heels clicking on the polished wood. She crossed her arms, her eyes trained on Amy.

"*You* don't deserve that pin," Chloe cried. "It *should* be my father's, and you all know it."

The members all shifted in their seats and turned away from Chloe to avoid her judgemental gaze. Amy adjusted the pin on her black cardigan, her spine stiffening.

"Emily would have wanted me to have it," Amy called out proudly. "Besides, I'm the only founding member left in the club."

"But not the only founding member in the village," Chloe said with a bitter laugh. "My father was the *first* member of this group. Yolanda wanted him to take over, but you all had different ideas."

"There's your motive right there!" Amy cried as she stumbled back, a finger pointing at Chloe. "You heard her. She wants her father to take over this club. That's the best motive I've heard so far."

Julia narrowed her eyes on Chloe, wondering if Amy could be right. The theory had crossed her mind after seeing the items on Chloe's backseat, but she had wanted to look the woman in the eyes before jumping to conclusions.

"Are you being serious?" Chloe cried with a strained laugh. "You don't believe this, do you?"

Chloe looked around the group, but they all avoided her eyes. She turned to Julia, but she also could not maintain eye contact. She was sure if she did, it would give her suspicions away in an instant. Chloe uncrossed her arms, and Julia noticed small scratches covering her fingers. She nudged Johnny and nodded to them. Had they been there when Julia had visited the cottage with the cake the day before? She could not remember.

"*Rose thorns!*" Johnny whispered, before turning to Chloe and puffing out his chest. "Where were you yesterday afternoon, Chloe?"

"I was at home."

"Can anybody prove that?" Johnny asked, his

pen poised over his notepad.

"Are you asking me for an alibi?" Chloe mumbled. "I don't have to listen to this. You people make me sick."

She turned on her heels and stormed out of the village hall. The doors slammed, sending a dull shudder through the room. The clicking of Brendan's camera was the only thing interrupting the silence.

"*She* did it!" Amy cried. "Chloe killed Margaret, Elsie, Edgar, and then she tried to kill Emily!"

"I *did* sense a darkness around her," Evelyn mumbled as she pulled a crystal from her pocket. "Such *darkness* for such a young woman."

"Why would she want to kill all of those people?" Mary cried, laughing as though she found the whole thing amusing.

"Because she wants her father to be president," Amy mumbled as she set off for the door. "And I'm the only one left to stand in his way. I need to go."

She ran across the hall and burst through the doors. Julia sighed, unsure of what to think. Amy's theory did make sense, but something just did not sit right with Julia. She felt like she was still missing a vital piece of the puzzle.

"Well, the show *must* go on." Mary stood up

and clapped her hands together. "We need to get some more texture shots for the magazine before the reveal on Saturday."

"It's still going ahead?" Julia asked. "Are you being serious?"

"We still have a magazine to produce," Mary mumbled as she scribbled something on her clipboard. "I think this is going to be our *best* issue yet. Come on, Brendan. I look forward to tasting your macarons, Julia. I heard they were delightful."

Mary also headed for the door, followed by Brendan who trailed behind snapping pictures of Julia and Johnny as he went. The club quickly descended into chaos without an obvious leader. The chatter rose until many separate arguments broke out in small clusters. Julia and Johnny left the suffocating village hall before the group turned on them too.

"What do we do now?" Johnny asked. "You've done this before."

"It's not like I go around solving murders on purpose," Julia said as they walked out of the church grounds. "I've never experienced anything this complicated before. We can't sit back and let this happen again."

"I need to get back to the office," Johnny said as

he checked his watch. "My editor is going to kill me. We're going to print with the Emily story tomorrow, and I haven't even started writing. I don't know where to start."

Julia looked across the village green at her café. Jessie was sweeping the doorstep, but it looked quiet inside.

"Can I come with you?" Julia asked, already heading for Johnny's car. "Tracing the killer's steps might unlock something."

CHAPTER 11

J ulia had never visited *The Peridale Post* offices
before, but she had always imagined they were
modest in size with a handful of employees.
When they drove out of Peridale and onto a small
industrial park with tall office buildings and
hundreds of cars parked there, Julia realised her
mental image could not have been more wrong.

"*This* is your office?" Julia whispered as she

climbed out of the car and looked up at the tall building with wide eyes.

"We only have the fourth floor. The entire building needs pulling down and rebuilding, but they're not about to do that for a dying platform. All of the newspapers from the surrounding villages work here too. Cotswold Media Group bought us all out a couple of years back and lumped us all together here. It was apparently easier and cheaper to have us all under one roof."

"Hardly the local operation that comes across in the paper."

"We try our best to keep it as authentic as possible," Johnny whispered as they passed a well-dressed man in a suit who nodded at him. "Not easy when you've got the men upstairs breathing down your neck about column inches and ad space. It's only a matter of time before they scrap the local news all together and just fill the paper with sponsored content."

They walked up the steps to the office building, which was impossibly dated. Like the village hall, it looked like it had been built in the 1970s, but its brutalist architecture and beige tiled walls had not aged as well.

They hurried through the scanners at the

entrance and towards the reception. Johnny flashed his badge at the lone woman behind the reception desk, but she did not look up from her copy of *Women's Weekly*. Johnny quickly scribbled Julia's name in a book on the desk and reached over the desk to grab a small white badge. He pinned the '*VISITOR*' badge to her cotton jumper, and they set off up the stairs.

"The lift stopped working last month," Johnny panted as they made their way past the third floor. "Said they were sending someone out to fix it, but I doubt that will ever happen. I don't even think they've made the call if I'm completely honest. We didn't have any working toilets on our floor until last week. We've been using the *Chedworth Gazette*'s on the fifth floor for years."

They reached the fourth floor, which was labelled '*The Peridale Post*' in a logo she had not seen on the front of the newspaper since she was a little girl. Julia followed Johnny through the double doors and into the open plan office.

"Alright, Johnny," a young man mumbled as he twirled chewing gum around his finger. "Who's the woman? Not from head office, is she?"

"You wish," Johnny said, knocking the man's feet off his desk as he walked by. "She's a villager."

"From Peridale?" the man called after them as they walked across the empty open office.

"Where else?" Johnny called back with a roll of his eyes. "The kid has never even been to the village."

"But he writes for *The Peridale Post*," Julia whispered as she hurried to keep up with Johnny. "How does that work?"

"Only the editor and I are from Peridale," Johnny said as he slowed down at an immaculately clean cubicle. "This is my desk. It's not much, but it's mine. I'm the last original journalist left after the group took over. The rest of them saw sense and jumped ship. They replaced a couple of the positions with people from within the company, but there aren't many of us left now. Readership is down across the area, but Peridale is still fighting strong compared to some of the others. I like to think that's because I spend half my life in the village to fill the pages with things people want to read, but maybe they're just buying out of habit."

"It's a good paper," Julia said as she looked around the sad and depressing empty office. "Despite everything."

"I'll take that as a compliment," Johnny said with a wink. "This is Rhonda's desk. This is where the obituaries have been appearing."

They walked to the cubicle on the other side of Johnny's. It was not as clean, but unlike Johnny's cubicle, the short walls were covered with family pictures. Julia did not recognise the woman who appeared in most of them, but she guessed that was because Rhonda was another woman working on the paper who had never been to Peridale.

"So, what you're telling me is, pretty much anybody can get into this building?" Julia asked with a sigh as she leaned against Rhonda's desk. "A building that is shared with a hundred other people."

"And one security camera," Johnny reminded her before turning and cupping his hands around his mouth and facing the young man at the front desk. "Josh? Have you gone through those videos like I asked?"

"On it, Johnny boy," Josh called back with a thumb in the air.

"*Useless,*" Johnny mumbled under his breath. "Do you see what I'm up against? I can't juggle everything, but I feel like I'm running this paper on my own. The editor is always up on the ninth floor with the design team. He thinks the layout is more important than the content. Haven't seen him down here in weeks. It's all email and cloud now."

"It sounds like you've fallen out of love with things," Julia suggested as she flicked through the paperwork on Rhonda's desk. "You still need passion."

"I have passion," Johnny said with a shrug. "I thrive when I'm sniffing out a story. There's always something going on in Peridale, you just need to listen. Besides, with all of these murders recently, I've had a lot to keep me busy."

"Maybe a little too busy?" Julia stepped back and stared down at the desk with the image of the killer planting the obituary in her mind. "When was the last time you went on a date?"

Johnny blushed as he pulled off his glasses. He squinted at Julia as he cleaned them on the edge of his blue shirt.

"Do you really want to know?" he asked with a half-smile. "When we went for coffee."

"But that was two years ago. You haven't been on a date since then?"

"It's not *that* long ago," he mumbled back as he pushed his glasses back up his nose. "I've been busy."

Julia squeezed his shoulder and gave him a reassuring smile. She did not like to think that Johnny was burying his head so much in his work that he was not living his life. She wanted him to find somebody like she had found Barker because he deserved better than his last date to be a quick coffee with a woman who had told him they were just great friends.

"There's only one door into this room," Julia affirmed, turning her attention back to the case. "So that eliminates the possibility of sneaking in. They'd have to walk through the front door. Pretty brave, don't you think? Do you think Josh knows anything?"

"I've already asked," Johnny said as he followed Julia back to the front of the office. "He's only part time anyway. Most of the people are. The office is empty most of the time if I'm not here."

Julia walked out of the doors and then walked back through them. She carefully traced the journey the culprit was likely to take. She tried to imagine what they were thinking as they made their way to Rhonda's desk to leave another obituary. Would they be excited, or nervous?

"They must have known that it was Rhonda who dealt with the obituaries," Julia theorised. "Or it was a good guess?"

"It's not hard to find out," Johnny said. "She's the person who replies personally to all of the families. But if they're getting in here, they probably knew this was her desk. There's no name tag."

"There's the pictures," Julia said. "But that would mean they needed to know what she looks like."

"A quick internet search would bring that up. How many Rhondas could there be in this area?"

"Good point." Julia tapped her finger on her chin as she paced back and forth. "So, they could know who she is, or they could have found out. They could have a pass, or they could have snuck in. We're getting *nowhere!*"

"Maybe we should take what we know about Chloe to the police?" Johnny suggested. "They might already be looking into her."

Julia stopped pacing to stare at Johnny. She knew he was right, but she hated not seeing the full picture. A can of oil and garden shears did not equal a murderer, even if a niggling voice told her it made the most sense. She was about to agree with him until something familiar tickled her nose. She inhaled deeply, the smell transporting her to a different time. She turned to face a closed door.

"What's in here?"

"Office stationary and cleaning stuff," Johnny said with a shrug. "I never really go in there."

Julia tried the brass doorknob, relieved when it opened. Her eyes lit up when she saw a thick, pink puddle next to a knocked over bottle. She crouched down and dipped her forefinger in the substance as she had done in Edgar's kitchen, but this time, she knew why she recognised the smell.

"We used this stuff when I worked in the cake factory back in London before I had my own café," Julia said as she rubbed the liquid between her fingers. "The smell would stick to your clothes."

"What is it?" Johnny asked as he picked up the sticky bottle.

"It's an industrial strength cleaner," she said as Johnny read over the label. "We used it to sterilise the floors and the equipment."

Julia found the light switch and flicked it on. The dim bulb did not make much difference, but it did illuminate boot prints Julia would have sworn were the same as the ones she had found at Edgar and Emily's cottages.

"They snuck in, planted the obituaries, and then came in here to hide before they could make their escape." Julia crouched down and picked up a big gloop of the liquid. She rolled it around in her hands and tried to shake it off. It did not move. "They unknowingly stood in this stuff and walked it back to the crime scenes. It only comes off with water, and it hasn't rained all month."

"But that doesn't tell us who did it," Johnny sighed as he flicked off the light. "Just that they were hiding in this cupboard. They were probably interrupted."

Julia knew Johnny was right, but she was satisfied that she had at least figured out one tiny part of the mystery. It felt like she was edging open the door and now that her foot was crammed in, it would only be a matter of time before she could blow the door fully open and bask in the light of the truth.

"Keep looking over that video footage," Julia said to Johnny as she stood up and looked down at her pink and sticky hands. "I need to get back to the café, but if you hear anything, let me know."

"What about Chloe?" Johnny asked. "What if she did do it?"

"What if she didn't?" Julia called over her shoulder as she pushed on the doors. "I might teach you a thing about investigative journalism yet, Johnny Watson."

Julia quickly washed her hands in the old and rundown bathroom before making her way downstairs. She called a taxi and waited on the side of the road, her mind whirring. She felt like the truth was staring her in the face, but her eyes were closed to it.

"What am I missing?" she mumbled to herself as the taxi pulled up in front of her. "What can't I see?"

CHAPTER 12

"More," Julia said, tipping up the bottom of the wine bottle as Barker poured it into her glass. "A bit more."

"I thought you weren't a drinker?" Barker asked as he emptied the wine into the glass.

"It's been a long week."

She settled into the couch, her feet toasting in

front of the fire. The sun was still setting on Peridale, but for Julia, the week had already ended. The grand prize reveal was tomorrow, and she was still no closer to figuring out who the murderer was. After another sip of her wine, she was not even sure if she cared anymore. The Green Fingers had drained every last ounce of her energy. She leaned and peeped at the three hundred macarons that were currently cooling on her kitchen counter. It was more than likely that they were contributing to her sudden change of mood.

"I still can't believe this charade is going ahead," Barker said after returning with a fresh bottle of chilled wine. "With Emily still in intensive care, I thought the magazine might postpone the celebrations until they at least knew if she was going to pull through."

"They want to throw their money at the winner so they can get out of here as soon as possible," Julia said after another sip of her wine. "I can't say I blame them."

Barker topped up his glass and added another splash in Julia's. She had only had one glass of wine, but it did not seem to be getting any emptier thanks to Barker's constant top-ups. She closed her eyes, the warm and fuzzy feeling prickling behind her eyes.

"I wonder if the deaths will stop when the magazine leaves," Julia thought aloud. "Or would it have happened regardless?"

"There's the sabotage too," Barker said. "That's fifteen gardens sabotaged in some way now. We can't keep up with the calls, but there's not a lot we can do. You can't charge somebody for the murder of a flower."

"Try telling that to Evelyn," Julia said with a girlish giggle. "She's probably holding a séance for her gardenias right this minute."

They chuckled behind their wine glasses like teenagers. She rested her head on Barker's shoulder and stared into the flickering flames. It would be so easy to close her eyes and drift off.

A small scream echoed from within the cottage, startling them both. Julia's wine glass wobbled, soaking her pyjama bottoms.

"What was that?" Barker whispered.

"It sounded like it came from Jessie's room." Julia pushed out of the deep couch. "Hold my glass."

Julia rubbed her temples as she wandered to Jessie's bedroom. She knocked softly before opening the creaky door. She popped her head in, surprised to see Jessie sat at her dressing table.

"Are you okay?" Julia whispered. "I heard a scream."

"It's nothing," Jessie said as she clutched her hands. "I burnt my hand on this *stupid* thing – It doesn't even matter."

Julia slipped into the bedroom and softly closed the door behind her. The distant sunset cast a warm wash across the messy teenager's room. Julia flicked on the bedside lamp and crept carefully towards Jessie.

"Where did you get that?" Julia asked, spotting the bright pink straightening iron on Jessie's dressing table.

"Sue gave them to me," Jessie said as she stared at Julia in the mirror, half her dark black hair straightened, and the other half its usual wavy frizz. "She said I should use them for – *never mind*."

"For what?"

Jessie chewed her lip as she stared at Julia in the mirror, the pink sunset filling her pale cheeks with colour. With her hair down and some of it straight, Julia saw a young woman staring back at her instead of a teenager.

"Billy wants to take me out," Jessie said, glancing at the clock on her nightstand. "He's coming in twenty minutes."

"And you're doing this for him?" Julia glanced at the straighteners, which looked as out of place in Jessie's bedroom as a large spotted elephant would. "You don't have to change for anyone, especially not a boy."

"But Sue said –"

"Sue says a lot of things." Julia chuckled as she leaned against Jessie's chair. "She's been trying to change me her entire life, and I let it go in one ear and out the other."

Julia picked up a paddle brush and began to brush through Jessie's hair. The un-straightened pieces were knotty, but she did not flinch as Julia pulled the brush through. They locked eyes in the mirror, sharing a smile that Julia only saw in these softer moments.

"If you want to straighten your hair, I can help you." Julia picked up the hot device and stared down at it in bewilderment. "I'm not saying I'll be any better at it than you, in fact, I might be worse, but I can help you get the back a bit better."

Jessie ran her fingers through the straight pieces framing her face. She observed herself in the mirror, her entire demeanour changing.

A lump suddenly rose in Julia's throat. She forced it down as she thought back to the sixteen-year-old girl with a dirty face and baggy clothes she had caught stealing from her café at the beginning of the year. She had known Jessie would not stay that girl forever, but she had naively never anticipated change so soon.

"It might be cool to see what it looks like straight," Jessie said with a shrug. "But it's for me, not him."

"Then that's all that matters." Julia smiled sweetly as she picked up the bottle of heat defence spray, which was also bright pink. "Between you and me, boys don't notice these things anyway. Now, let me see if I can remember how to do this."

Julia took the hair in small sections and ran a comb through before ironing it flat. She worked around the head, transforming Jessie's frizzy locks to a shiny and sleek style. Julia's mind wandered to losing her own mother and all of the experiences she had been denied. Would they have done these things together? Julia smiled to herself, knowing that it did not matter. She could not change the past, but she was here doing this for Jessie.

When Julia was finished, she pushed the hair over Jessie's shoulders and crouched down so that their faces were level in the mirror.

"You look beautiful," Julia whispered with a

squeeze of her shoulders.

Jessie looked up at her reflection, her eyes widening. She frowned a little as she turned her head from side to side, not seeming to recognise herself. Julia could not believe what a difference such a small change could make.

"I look like one of those girls," Jessie whispered as she ran her fingers through her hair. "Dolly and Dom would freak if they saw me like this."

"I won't tell them if you don't," Julia whispered with a wink. "What time did you say Billy was getting here?"

Before Jessie could answer, there was a small knock on the front door. Butterflies flooded through Julia's stomach, but they were not her own. She was feeling them for Jessie in a way she had never experienced before.

"I'm not sure if I like it," Jessie whispered as she pushed her face into the mirror.

"Billy won't care what you look like." Julia kissed Jessie on the top of the head. "I'll stall him while you finish getting ready."

Jessie smiled her thanks as she rested her hand on Julia's. They stayed there for a moment before Julia turned and headed for the door. She was scared if she had not, she might not have been able to force down the lump in her throat again. She blamed it on the wine, but she knew it was more than that.

Julia slipped out of Jessie's bedroom, the overpowering stench of aftershave suffocating her.

"*Billy*," Julia croaked as she wafted her hand in front of her nose. "You look – *nice*."

Billy looked down at the suit that was three times too big for him. Julia had not seen him wearing anything other than trainers and tracksuits, and from how uncomfortable Billy looked, neither had he.

"Are you sure?" Billy slicked back his usually unruly hair. "It's my dad's court suit."

"The aftershave his too?" Barker asked through a cough, his eyes watering.

"I borrowed a splash," Billy announced proudly as he held his wrist out for Barker to smell. "He got it off the market really cheap. I think it fell off the back of a truck, if you get my drift."

"I can smell it from here," Barker said with a forced smile. "I think the whole of Peridale gets your drift."

Julia shot Barker a look that read '*play nice*', before sending a soothing smile in Billy's direction. She remembered how nerve-wracking it was to date at that age. She had thrown up before her first date and had forced Sue to phone and cancel for her.

"Can I get you a drink while you wait?" Julia asked, rubbing her hands together. "I've got orange juice, or maybe some water?"

"Have you got beer?"

"You're seventeen," Barker mumbled.

"*So?*" Billy mumbled with an arch of his brow. "Been drinking for years."

"Orange juice it is," Julia said with a cheery smile. "Barker, why don't you join me in the kitchen while Billy makes himself comfortable on the couch."

Julia dragged Barker into the kitchen. They both clamped their hands over their mouths as they suppressed their laughter. Julia pushed open the kitchen window, the smell somehow having followed her in.

"Be nice," Julia said with a slap on Barker's arm. "He's trying to be a gentleman."

"Most gentlemen don't have criminal records, and they certainly don't have to borrow their dad's court suit."

Julia pulled the orange juice from the fridge and quickly poured a glass. She kissed Barker on the forehead before she took it through. Billy was sitting in the middle of the couch reading over the wine label.

"My mum drinks this stuff," Billy said as he set it down on the coffee table next to Julia and Barker's wine glasses. "Gets a good deal on it down the cash and carry."

Julia had only met Billy's mother once, but she had not left a very good impression. She was a chain-smoking woman who lived on the less than fortunate Fern Moore Estate with her two other kids, both of whom had different dads to Billy. Julia did not know the woman, so she tried not to unfairly judge her. She knew there was a chance, even if it was slim, that Billy's mother might one day become Jessie's mother-in-law.

Billy downed his orange juice in one gulp, turning swiftly as Jessie's bedroom door opened. He quickly stood up and wiped his lips with his overhanging sleeve.

"*Wow!*" Billy's eyes lit up as he looked Jessie up and down. "You look – *different.*"

"Is that your dad's suit?" Jessie asked awkwardly as she teetered forward, an uncharacteristic shyness taking over her.

"It's his court suit," Barker answered for him with a knowing nod as he walked into the sitting room. "Jessie, you look – *different.*"

Macarons and Mayhem

Jessie looked down at her outfit as Julia tried to think of another word to describe her new look, but she could not. She did look different. Julia had never seen her wearing anything other than shades of black and grey, but she had replaced her baggy jeans with a pair of figure-hugging pale blue jeans. Her black hoody had been substituted for a white t-shirt tucked casually into the jeans. A small leather jacket covered her shoulders, and matching leather boots with chunky gold heels were on her feet. She wobbled on them as she tucked her sleek hair behind her ears.

"Sue took me shopping," she said defensively, a frown creasing her brow.

"You look beautiful," Julia assured her.

"Yeah," Billy and Barker chimed together. "*Beautiful.*"

Jessie smiled shyly and let her straight hair fall over her face. She looked at Billy with wide eyes and red cheeks, and then to the door. He nodded and hurried around the sofa.

"Don't be too late," Julia called after them. "I'll leave the door on the latch."

Jessie did not respond as she opened the front door. Julia could feel her eagerness to leave and get out into the fresh air, but Barker had other ideas. He grabbed Billy's arm before he could follow her out.

"You better look after her," Barker whispered down at the young man. "Or you'll have me to deal with."

"I will," Billy said as he brushed Barker's hand away. "Chill out, Detective Inspector. I like her, alright?"

"Good," Barker said, holding his hands up. "Where are you taking her?"

"Gonna go to Krusty's Chicken near the estate," he announced proudly. "They do the best –"

"No," Barker said, reaching into his pocket to pull out his wallet. "Here's thirty quid. Take her to The Comfy Corner. It's Spicy Friday, and she loves the Vindaloo. Here's a word of advice for you, kid. If a girl dresses up like that, don't take her to Krusty's Chicken. I don't care if they have the best chicken wraps in the whole world."

Billy saluted to Barker, pocketed the cash with a grin, and followed Jessie out of the cottage. Barker closed the door behind him, leaving it on the latch like Julia had promised.

"You keep making me love you more and more." Julia wrapped her arms around Barker's neck. "Just when I think I know you, you surprise me."

"I need to keep you on your toes," he whispered

before kissing her.

They stumbled back, and Julia fell into the couch. They toppled onto the cushions, giggling behind their pressed lips. Julia edged up the couch, her head banging on something solid.

"*Ouch!*" Julia cried out as something crashed down to the ground. "What was that?"

She wriggled out from under Barker and looked over the edge. Her heart stopped when she saw that it was Barker's briefcase and that the crash to the ground had sprung open the lock. She scrambled to her feet, scooped up as many of the papers as she could, and ran into the kitchen.

"'*Julia was a brave and smart woman, with a tongue of steel and the confidence to match*'," Julia read aloud from the page full of text. "'*She was the type of woman you didn't know you wanted in your life until she was there. That was why I trusted her judgement when it came to the Gertrude Smith case*'."

"*Julia!*" Barker cried as he chased after her. "Give that back."

"What is this?" she asked with a laugh. She flicked through the papers, her name popping up on every page. "Are these case notes?"

"Do they look like case notes?" he replied with blushing cheeks. "It's – It's *embarrassing*."

"Tell me," Julia said as she passed the paper back. "I'm not going to laugh."

"I'm -," Barker's voice broke off as he looked down at the paper again. "I'm writing a book, okay?"

"A book?" Julia exclaimed.

"You said you wouldn't laugh!"

"*I'm not*!" Julia cried. "I'm just a little shocked, that's all. You're writing a book?"

Barker nodded as he straightened out the paper. He could barely look Julia in the eyes.

"It's always been a dream of mine," he said, almost apologetically. "Ever since I was a kid in school. It's stupid."

"It's not stupid," Julia said. "You've written about me in your book?"

"I'm writing about the Gertrude Smith case," he said with a shrug. "My first case in the village, and the case that brought us together."

"And the case *I* solved," Julia reminded him. "Wait, did I just read that you trusted my judgement? That's not how I remember it happening, Barker. You told me to stay out, and you underestimated me at every turn."

"It's called creative licence," he said with a small smirk. "I read about it online. It means you can stretch the truth and mould things. I should have trusted your judgement at the time, so now I am in fiction."

Julia looked down at the paper, unsure of what to think. Pride swelled in her chest, but she could not believe Barker had not wanted to tell her. Even she shared her less than successful bakes with him for constructive criticism.

"Can I read it?"

"It's not finished." He walked back into the sitting room. "It's a rough draft. It needs a lot of work."

"I'd still like to read it."

"You can," he said as he stuffed the papers into the briefcase. "Just not yet. Is that Amy?"

Barker stood up and pulled back the net curtains. Julia joined him, the light from her sitting room illuminating the lane as the last of the sun drifted from the sky. She squinted into the dark and watched as a familiar pale pink cardigan bent over in front of Emily's front door.

Julia did not hang around. She pushed her feet into her sheepskin slippers, pulled her dressing gown across her pyjamas and hurried down her own garden path. When she saw that Amy was laying a bouquet of red roses in front of Emily's cottage, Julia slowed down and hung back as Amy sobbed into a handkerchief. After almost a minute of watching the woman cry, Julia cleared her throat.

"*Julia?*" Amy squinted into the dark. "What are you doing out here? In your pyjamas too!"

"I saw you from my cottage." Julia stepped under the crime scene tape strapped across Emily's garden gate. "Isn't it a little late to be bringing flowers?"

"I've just been to the hospital," Amy said with a stifled cry. "The doctor told me she might never wake up, and if she does, she might have – she *might* have permanent brain damage. It's *awful!* It's going to take a miracle."

Amy thrust herself into Julia's arms and wrapped herself around her. She comforted the old woman and rubbed her fluffy cardigan as she sobbed on her shoulder.

"She's a tough old cookie," Julia whispered as she looked around at the shrivelling rose petals strewn all over the garden. "I'm sure she'll pull through."

"It's all my fault," Amy mumbled as she pulled away and wiped her red nose. "I could have stopped all of this from happening at the beginning. Oh, Julia, we did a terrible thing, and now we're being punished for it."

"What did you do?" Julia asked, grabbing Amy's shoulders and staring her dead in the eyes. "Tell me what you did. We can stop this now."

Amy opened her mouth as though she was going to reveal everything Julia had suspected she had known all along, but she clamped her lips shut and pulled away from Julia. She hurried back down the garden path and thrust through the crime scene tape, yanking it off her as she scurried down the winding lane and back towards the village.

"She knows something, Barker," Julia whispered after walking back to her cottage. "She said '*they*' did something terrible."

"Who are '*they*'?" he replied.

"I don't know," Julia sighed with frustration. "Amy and Emily? The Green Fingers? Someone else entirely? I'm so close to the truth, I can feel it."

"Well, there's nothing you can do about it tonight," Barker said, taking Julia's hands and pulling her back to the couch. "Jessie will be out for the rest of the evening, and I think we were in the middle of something before you decided to bust open my briefcase."

CHAPTER 13

Julia looked out of her café window at the large white tent on the village green as she poured a shot of espresso into a latte. Despite everything that had happened, there was an excited buzz in the village, and from the unknown faces of the customers in Julia's café, word of the grand prize reveal had spread beyond the Peridale border.

"I got here as quickly as I could," Sue said as she

hurried through the café red-faced. "I couldn't find anywhere to park."

Sue pecked Julia on the cheek and hurried around the counter to grab an apron, which rested nicely on her bump. Julia had called her first thing that morning when she had seen how many people were milling around the white tent in the heart of the village. A small part of Julia had assumed people would stay away considering the recent deaths, but it seemed to have had the opposite effect.

"There are TV cameras out there!" Dot exclaimed as she pushed through the tourists to bring her pot of tea to the counter. "Looks like they're talking to Amy. Maybe I should go out there and get myself on the box. I am an *official* member, after all."

"I've told you that you don't need to bother with that, Gran," Julia said. "I don't even know what I thought you would find."

"It's better than sitting at home," Dot said with a shrug. "Besides, it's *rather* entertaining. All of that arguing really does get the blood pumping. I join in, and I don't even know what they're arguing about half of the time. It's *quite* exciting."

Dot pulled a small compact mirror from her handbag and checked her roller-set grey curls before pushing her way towards the door, no doubt to wrestle Amy away from the TV cameras.

"We're out of wholemeal bread," Jessie called from the kitchen. "And we're getting low on butter too."

Julia grabbed a ten-pound note from the petty cash tin and let Sue take over behind the till. She pushed through the growing line forming in front of the counter and burst out of the café into the summer heat. Shielding her eyes from the sun, she looked across the village green and into the open white tent. Mary and Brendan were talking in front of the tables containing three hundred of Julia's multi-coloured macarons. Brendan said something, which caused Mary to cackle loudly. They both looked in the direction of the TV camera and interviewer, who were interviewing Amy outside the closed Happy Bean coffee shop. Dot lingered in the back of the shot, pacing back and forth and ignoring the interviewer who was trying to shoo her away.

"Just these, please, Shilpa," Julia said as she put three loaves of wholemeal bread and a tub of butter on the counter. "Lovely day out."

"And yet I can't wait for it to be over," she said lightly as she accepted Julia's money. "That magazine has brought nothing but bad karma to our village. It wasn't what Yolanda would have wanted."

"Maybe all of this would have happened differently if Yolanda had still been here," Julia suggested as she took her change. "I guess we'll never know."

"Emily certainly made sure all of this happened *her* way." Shilpa loaded the bread into a plastic bag. "I visited her this morning. Took her some flowers. Claims she doesn't remember a thing about what happened to her."

"She's awake?"

"Woke up in the early hours," Shilpa said with a strained smile. "She looked so weak. It was easy to forget she was just a little old woman when she was bossing us around."

"She's going to be okay?" Julia asked.

"It seems like it," Shilpa said with a nod as she handed over the bag. "I suppose that's one blessing to come out of all of this."

"I suppose it is," Julia mumbled. "I'd better get back to the café."

Julia walked to the door in a daze. She had almost accepted what Amy had said about Emily possibly never waking up, or never being the same again. Despite everything that had happened, Emily did not deserve to die.

Dread replaced Julia's relief as she walked out into the bright sun again. With all the excitement in the air, it was almost easy to pretend everything was going to be fine, even if the murderer was still out there. Julia cast an eye in Amy's direction, knowing she could very well be next.

"*Julia!*" Johnny cried as he ran towards her, a camera around his neck and a notepad in his hand. "I've been looking everywhere for you. Emily's awake."

"I heard," Julia said, hooking her thumb over her shoulder at the post office. "Apparently she doesn't remember a thing."

"I've just been to see her. She's still in a bad way, but she doesn't remember who hit her. I was hoping she would at least give me something to put an end to all of this, but she claims the last thing she remembers is watering her roses and walking back into her cottage. Have you thought any more about going to the police about Chloe?"

Julia opened her mouth to speak, but she was distracted when she saw Mercy pushing Peter across the village, both of them avoiding looking in the direction of the white tent. Peter was holding a giant bouquet of white lilies in his lap, no doubt bought from Pretty Petals. Johnny turned around and followed Julia's eye line to the father and daughter.

"Today must be hard for them," Johnny said after he sucked the air through his teeth. "This whole event was Yolanda's doing, and she's not even here to enjoy it."

"And she's not the only one," Julia whispered, thinking about Margaret, Elsie, and Edgar. "I need to get back to the café. It's packed. I can't leave Sue on her own."

"I need to take some pictures for the paper anyway," Johnny said with a pat on his camera. "Work comes first."

"Did Josh find anything on the security footage?" Julia asked, suddenly remembering the newspaper office.

"Nobody that shouldn't have been there," he said with a defeated shrug. "Maybe they did scale the walls after all."

"Maybe," Julia said with a chuckle. "I'll see you later."

Julia set off back to her café, but she let out a yelp when a hand closed around her arm and dragged her into the shadowy alley between her café and the post office.

"*Evelyn?*" Julia cried out, her heart pounding. "What are you doing?"

Evelyn pulled Julia deep into the alley, only stopping when they were behind Julia's car and hidden from view. Evelyn let go of Julia's arm and adjusted her red turban as she chomped on her lips.

"I'm sorry," Evelyn whispered. "I can't risk anyone seeing."

Evelyn reached into her pocket and pulled out a small blue crystal. She squeezed it between her hands before pressing her lips against it. She lifted it to the sky and whispered something to herself before passing the crystal to Julia and closing her fingers around it.

"For protection," Evelyn explained. "We need to be safe."

"Have you been on the Tibetan tea?" Julia asked as she looked awkwardly down at the glittering crystal. "Why don't you come into my café? I'll get Jessie to make you a nice sandwich, and you can have a scone. I know how much you like them."

"I haven't been drinking the tea," Evelyn whispered, a devious smile flickering across her lips for a moment. "But Amy has."

Julia frowned down at the little eccentric woman, wondering what on earth she was talking about. She decided to lean against the bonnet of her car and listen to what she had to say.

"Amy came to my B&B late last night," Evelyn explained. "She was distraught, so I gave her a little Tibetan tea to relax her, and – *well*, she had a slight *adverse* reaction to it."

"You mean your hallucinogenic tea *didn't* relax her?" Julia asked sarcastically.

"Shocking, I know," Evelyn replied seriously. "I think she must have been allergic. She started rocking in the corner of the room. She said she could see *Yolanda*! I sensed her spirit anyway, so I lit some candles and pulled out the Ouija board. We spoke to her for hours. She told me to tell you that she appreciates you trying to help."

Julia forced herself to not roll her eyes. She exhaled heavily through her nostrils and pinched between her eyes with her free hand. Glancing to her café wall, she passed the crystal back to Evelyn.

"I appreciate you thinking I might want to hear this, but I'm really busy, and –"

"That's not all," Evelyn whispered, her excited smile growing. "The tea has a habit of *loosening* people's tongues. When we finished the séance, Amy told me what they did to force Yolanda out of the group."

Julia's ears suddenly pricked up. She stood up straight and stared at Evelyn, her heart pounding in her chest.

"Okay?" Julia urged. "What did she say?"

Evelyn gulped as she glanced over Julia's shoulder at the opening of the alley. The village buzzed as the crowds thickened, but they could not be seen from their position. Evelyn still dragged her deeper into the dark.

"Emily had always wanted to be president of the group," Evelyn started in a low whisper. "I knew it, Yolanda knew it, and everyone else knew it, but we also knew it was never going to happen while Yolanda was alive. We all agreed it was her group and it would stay that way until she didn't want it anymore."

"The thing was, Emily knew that day was never going to come, so she organised a mutiny against Yolanda's leadership. Amy claims that Emily spoke to each of the founding members and convinced them all to vote against Yolanda in the next meeting so they could elevate Emily."

"How did she do that?" Julia asked.

"*Blackmail*," Evelyn whispered with a swish of her arms from under her kaftan. "She used whatever she could find out about the members against them. According to Amy, Emily had been watching and listening for *years*, gathering as much information as she could. Margaret and Elsie were a little *more* than friends after their husbands died, if you know what I'm saying, and Edgar was using illegal chemicals to enhance his garden."

"I thought that was Malcolm?"

"Emily knew she could never use anything against Malcolm. He loved Yolanda too much, but she knew she didn't need him. With the rest of the group onside, she had a majority. She took Edgar's chemicals and claimed she found them in Malcolm's cottage."

"What did she use against Amy?"

"Nothing," Emily said. "What is there to use? We all know Amy spent decades in prison after being a bank robber. She's an open book, and Emily knew that. She offered her something."

"What?"

"*Power*," Evelyn whispered, her eyes lighting up. "She said if Amy went along with it, she would make Amy her vice president and she would have influence in the group. Yolanda never bothered with that. It was supposed to be fun, but Emily always took it too seriously. She never stopped talking about her roses, and now look at them."

"This is all really useful," Julia whispered as she made mental notes of everything she had just heard.

"There's more."

"More?"

"The night Emily carried out her revolt was the night Yolanda crashed her car and died." Evelyn paused to gulp as she adjusted her turban. "She was so distraught, she went to The Plough to drown her sorrows. She always liked her rum, but she must have been heartbroken to get that drunk. These people were her friends, and they turned on her to protect their secrets and gain power. They didn't crash the car for her, but they as good as killed her."

Julia's hand drifted up to her mouth as she let the words soak in. She could not believe the lengths Emily had gone to for the sake of a pin and a title in a small village group.

"That explains why it's only the founding members who are being targeted," Julia thought aloud. "But how does the murderer know? Emily would have made sure that nobody ever told her little secret."

"Maybe Amy told someone else?"

"Maybe," Julia said, although she did not believe Amy would be as loose-lipped without Evelyn's special tea to guide her. "I need to go."

Julia did not give Evelyn the option of continuing her story. She turned on her heels and hurried down the alley. Instead of going to her café, she headed in the opposite direction to The Plough.

Every seat outside of the small pub was filled, and the inside was just as bad. Julia fought her way through the drinking crowd to the bar.

"*Shelby!*" she called across the bar to the landlady. "Shelby, I need to ask you something."

"I'm a little busy right now, Julia," Shelby cried back without looking up from the pint she was pulling. "My useless son is upstairs with the flu, and my even more useless husband decided it was a good time to go away on a fishing trip with the boys."

She handed over a pint to the man she was serving and accepted his money before moving onto the next customer. Julia waited until she made her way down to her side of the bar.

"I need to ask you about Yolanda Turner," Julia said in a low voice, not wanting to catch the attention of unwanted ears. "I need to know about the night she crashed her car."

Shelby met Julia's eyes for the first time, and it became obvious it was an uncomfortable situation for her.

"If I'd have known she was driving, I never would have let her leave," Shelby mumbled as she handed over another pint. "She liked her rum, but she was knocking it back like it was her job that night. I just assumed she would get a taxi. I never thought she was that stupid."

"Did you see anyone in here with her?" Julia asked.

"She was on her own for most of the night, but she was speaking to a young woman," Shelby said as she moved onto the man next to Julia. "I'd never seen her before, and she didn't stay long. She tried to get Yolanda to go with her, but she wouldn't."

"Do you know who she was?" Julia asked. "Did you recognise her?"

"I only know the faces of people who buy drinks in my pub," Shelby said quickly, clearly becoming irritated by Julia's questions and the growing rabble in her pub. "I asked her if she wanted a drink and she told me she didn't drink alcohol, so I tossed her onto the useless pile in my brain. Sorry I can't be more useful, but I need to get on."

"You've been more than useful," Julia whispered, almost to herself. "I think I know who it is. I know who is killing the Green Fingers."

CHAPTER 14

J ulia hurried out of The Plough, her heart pounding in her chest. The bright sun bounced off a passing car, blinding her as she looked ahead at the police station. Her thoughts toppled over each other, all the tiny details slotting together like a perfectly formed jigsaw. Despite what she had figured out, she knew it was not enough to run into the station with; they would think she was a babbling lunatic.

"*Johnny!*" Julia ran forward when she saw the journalist leaving the post office with a bottle of water. "Johnny, I've figured it out!"

"Figured what out?" he asked after taking a sip.

"I know who the murderer is," she said, almost unable to contain her grin. "But just to be sure, does the newspaper hire Peridale Cleaning Company to clean the office?"

"They clean the whole building." Johnny frowned at her, clearly not joining together the same dots Julia had. "How did you know?"

Julia opened her mouth to explain, but ear-piercing static crackled through the village.

"*Thank you all for coming today,*" Mary's voice sizzled through giant speakers. "*Cotswold Gardening Magazine has had an interesting experience during our time in Peridale. It's certainly one we won't forget in a hurry.*"

The villagers and tourists crowded around Mary at the opening of the white tent. Brendan clutched a giant novelty cheque behind him, which caused more than a few excited smiles from the villagers. Julia and Johnny glanced at each other before joining the back of the crowd.

"You all know why we're here today," Mary boomed out, forced positivity loud in her voice. "We aren't just here to take pictures and write about your *charming* village, we are also here to discover the best garden in Peridale. And of course, the recipient of the title will win a cool *ten thousand pounds*, which I suspect is what brought most of you here today!"

There was a small cheer for the money, mainly from the Green Fingers, who were gathered at the front of the crowd. Amy seemed to be the only one not excited about the prize. Julia wondered if that was because her garden had been destroyed before being judged, or because her mind was still firmly fixed on Emily.

"Are you going to tell me who did all of this?" Johnny whispered into Julia's ear as Mary rattled off facts about the magazine. "Shouldn't we be going to the police?"

Julia opened her mouth to speak, but Malcolm and Chloe Johnson caught her eye as they walked arm in arm towards the crowd. Malcolm chomped down on his nails, and it looked like Chloe was dragging him. Chloe whispered something to her father, and it seemed to ease him a little. He looked around the large crowd, his eyes landing on Julia. He gave her a small smile, which she returned uneasily.

"*Julia?*" Johnny whispered. "Are you even listening to me?"

"I'll be back in a minute."

Julia left Johnny and walked towards Chloe and Malcolm. She did not know what she was going to say to them, but she knew she needed to say something. Malcolm waved in her direction, and she almost waved back, until she realised he was looking past her. Julia turned around and watched as Mercy pushed Peter towards them. Julia stepped to the side and merged into the crowd again. She watched out of the corner of her eyes as Peter and Malcolm shook hands. Mercy and Chloe acknowledged each other, but they did not speak.

Julia separated from the crowd again and set off across the village green towards the group. She thought she had got to know each of them in some way since Johnny had brought the deaths to her attention. As she stared at the murderer, she realised she did not know them at all.

"We only came to see who got the prize," Julia heard Chloe whisper as she got closer. "Since Emily croaked it, I'm more than a little intrigued to find out who has the best garden in Peridale if it isn't my father."

"Emily isn't dead," Peter whispered back. "At

least, that's what I heard."

"She isn't?" Malcolm replied, sounding a little stunned. "I thought she was hit pretty hard."

"She was," Mercy replied. "She's tougher than she looks."

Julia thought about what she was going to say to the group as she approached them. She knew outing the murderer would likely result in laughter and denial. If there was a way to get the murderer to confess and admit their crimes, she had to think of it and quickly.

A police car skidded to a halt right beside them. The people at the back of the crowd turned to stare at the sudden appearance of authority. Julia's heart skipped a beat in her chest when she saw Barker jump out of the passenger side of the car.

"There she is, boss," the uniformed officer cried, pointing at the group in front of Julia. "I *knew* it was her."

The young officer pulled handcuffs from his belt as Barker jogged to catch up with him. Malcolm and Peter looked uneasily at each other, but the women didn't react. It was almost as though neither of them thought the police could be there for them.

"*Chloe Johnson?*" the officer called out as he shielded the bright sun from his eyes with his free hand. "Can we have a word, please?"

"*A word?*" she snapped back with a small laugh. "What could I have *possibly* done that you need to speak to me? Are those handcuffs?"

Chloe's cries caught the attention of most of the crowd, including Mary, whose voice suddenly trailed off over the speakers.

"What's she done?" a man shouted from the crowd.

Barker caught Julia's eyes and gave her a look that she knew meant '*stay out of it*'. She shook her head to let him know he was about to make a huge mistake, but he turned away and pressed on.

"Chloe Johnson, you're under arrest for vandalising fifteen gardens." Barker's voice boomed as he nodded to the young officer to cuff her. "You're also under arrest for the murders of Margaret Harwood, Elsie Davies, Edgar Partridge, and the attempted murder of Emily Burns."

A horrified gasp shuddered through the crowd, the whispering stopping in an instant. Mary's gasp echoed through the microphone and out of the speakers. Chloe recoiled as she stared at her father, and then at the officer as he walked towards her with cuffs. She looked like she did not know whether to laugh or cry.

"There's been a mistake," she cried, her voice cracking as her bottom lip trembled. "I didn't kill anyone."

"We have several security clips of you vandalising gardens around the village," Barker said smugly. "Including one of you tossing oil over Evelyn's garden, which was caught on the crystal clear police station cameras, and from another angle on The Plough's camera for good measure. I've also got a clip of your car driving to and from Emily Burns' cottage around the time she would have been attacked, thanks to my own personal security cameras outside my cottage. Once we knew we were looking for you, you cropped up all over the village."

"I – *I* – " Chloe mumbled as the officer dragged her hands behind her back. "*I didn't kill anyone.*"

"But you admit to vandalising the gardens?" Amy cried, bursting forward from the crowd, her pin glittering under the sun. "You sneaky – "

"It's what you all *deserved!*" Chloe cried, spit flying from her snarled lips. "None of you have a right to win that money. My father has the best garden in Peridale."

Barker read Chloe her rights as she screamed and ranted. Julia tried to get Barker's attention again, but he seemed to be purposefully ignoring her.

"You've got the *wrong* person," Julia cried out, her voice drowning in the sea of chatter. "Barker! Chloe *didn't* kill those people."

The young officer pulled Chloe towards the police car regardless. She kicked and screamed, thrashing against him with all of her might, her blonde bob flying from side to side. Malcolm stood by and watched, his mouth ajar. Glistening beads of sweat dripped down his forehead. She could not stand by and watch Chloe get arrested for two crimes when she only committed one of them.

Julia pushed her fingers up into her hair. She looked desperately around her for a way to catch Barker's attention. She thought about throwing herself on the bonnet of the car, or standing in its way so they could not drive to the station, but she knew Barker would not hesitate in arresting her if he needed to.

She looked back at Johnny, who was snapping every moment of the unfolding arrest. Julia rolled her eyes, knowing he would not be any use. She looked over at the white tent, a spark of inspiration igniting.

After pushing through the thick and reluctant crowd, she snatched the microphone from Mary, who seemed too stunned to stop her. Dot looked at

Julia from the gathered Green Fingers, her mouth dropping.

"*Chloe didn't kill those people*," Julia called out, her voice commanding everyone's attention over the speakers. "I know that's what it looks like."

Every pair of eyes turned back to the tent and stared at her. The whispering stopped immediately, and she even noticed Barker holding his hand up to stop the officer pushing Chloe into the car. With the entire village waiting on her next words, Julia gulped down the rising nerves and tried to clear her mind. She thought about everything she had figured out since Evelyn's ambush and her visit to The Plough. How could she have missed all of the clues?

"Chloe didn't kill those people," Julia repeated again. "But I know who did. I don't doubt Chloe vandalised those gardens, including Emily's on the day she was attacked. She might even have massacred the roses while Emily lay bleeding inside, but who could have blamed her? After everything Emily did to the club and Chloe's father."

"Who killed them, Julia?" Dot cried, enticing the crowd to ask the same question. "Tell us what you know."

The chatter rose again as they all started to ask the same question, their sceptical gazes trained on

Julia. Flashes from Johnny's camera made her blink, derailing her train of thought.

"The person who killed Margaret, Elsie, Edgar, and tried to kill Emily, moved around this village completely unseen," Julia started, her thoughts gathering again. "They could go from *The Peridale Post* offices, where they were leaving obituaries to let us know the Green Fingers were being targeted, and then they could commit the crimes without being seen. They planned out each murder perfectly so they didn't leave behind a scrap of evidence. They pushed their victims down the stairs, and resorted to hitting them over the head when they didn't have stairs, no doubt with gloved hands I suspect. They were so good, that it took me longer than I would have liked to connect the dots. I didn't even realise the significance of the one clue they left behind until today.

"I heard Edgar's murder, and I was the first on the scene. I saw pink footprints in his kitchen, and again in Emily's. The smell was familiar to me, but it wasn't until this week that I realised the pink footprints were caused by a rather sticky industrial cleaning product. A cleaning product used by Peridale Cleaning Company. Some of you probably know the company. They probably clean your houses and your businesses. I know I've seen their branded cars all over the village. That's how the killer went unseen and how they moved around. That's why nobody noticed you, isn't it, Mercy?"

There was a gasp as all heads whipped to look at the former Green Fingers' president's daughter. Mercy looked down at her father, and then up at Julia, her bright eyes wide and unblinking.

"I'm sorry to say this, Peter, but it was your daughter who pushed those people down the stairs and hit Emily over the head." Julia paused to take a breath. "She's a murderer, and even though I don't condone what she did, I understand."

"Why would she do such a thing?" Mary asked, stepping forward as she peered into the crowd with a hand over her eyes. "It doesn't add up."

"For revenge," Julia said. "Mercy was the only person who knew that Emily had blackmailed all of the founding members of the club to banish Yolanda as their leader. She knew this because she visited her mother in the pub, where Yolanda told her everything that had happened, right before Yolanda crashed her car and died."

Mercy folded her arms over her blue apron and looked down at the ground, avoiding her father's eyes. He looked at her open-mouthed and stunned.

"When Shelby said the young woman who spoke to Yolanda in the pub didn't drink, all of the other pieces slotted together," Julia said with a soft sigh. "Peter, you were so proud that your daughter was a good girl. Remember when we were at Malcolm's cottage and you told me she didn't drink alcohol?

"The final piece of the puzzle came when I asked Johnny what cleaning company the newspaper used. I might not have made the connection if I hadn't helped Mercy pack her supplies away after cleaning Barker's cottage. I'm so sorry, but *you* killed those people. You blamed them for your mother's death. They might not have driven the car for her, but them stabbing her in the back drove her to drown her sorrows and make the fatal decision that ended her life."

Julia dropped the microphone to her side and stared across the crowd at Mercy. Julia smiled apologetically at the woman. Despite everything, she was still empathetic towards her.

"They were her *friends!*" Mercy screamed, pointing at Amy. "She *trusted* you!"

Amy couldn't bring herself to look at Mercy. She stumbled back and turned around, fleeing to the safety of her club.

"*Mercy?*" Peter mumbled, looking up at his daughter with tears in his eyes. "Please tell me all of this isn't true?"

"You should have heard her, Dad," Mercy whispered, glossy tears tumbling down her eyes. "The night she died, she was so heartbroken. If they hadn't turned their backs on her, she would still be here. She was so pure, and she adored that group and everything it stood for, and all they wanted to do was get rid of her. *They* killed her. All of this is *their* fault."

Dot suddenly shuffled away from the group, her hands in the air. She joined Julia by her side and wrapped her hand around her shoulder.

"I told you I never liked gardening," Dot whispered.

They both walked back through the crowd, which parted like the Red Sea, their eyes fixed disbelievingly on Julia. When she reached Mercy, all Julia could do was give the young woman a hug.

"I had hoped I was wrong," Julia whispered into her ear. "Take care of yourself."

Julia rested her hand on Peter's shoulder as the young officer scrambled to unlock Chloe's handcuffs.

"Mercy Turner, you're under arrest for the

murders of Margaret Harwood, Elsie Davies, Edgar Partridge, and the attempted murder of Emily Burns."

Barker read his cleaner her rights as she stared silently at the floor. Unlike Chloe, she did not thrash or fight, she accepted her defeat with grace and dignity. She mouthed her apologies to her father before walking to the police car.

"I can't believe you figured all of that out from some pink slime and a pub conversation," Johnny said as he joined her. "I could barely keep up scribbling all of that down. It's certainly going to make a juicy issue of the paper."

"Can you promise me you'll do one thing?" Julia asked him.

"Anything."

"Leave my name out of it," she said with an exhausted laugh as she planted a hand on his shoulder. "Please?"

Johnny looked down at his notes. He thought about it for a moment before crossing something out and winking at Julia.

"Consider it done," Johnny said. "Although most of the villagers are here, so I don't know what difference it'll make."

The police car drove away with Mercy in the

back. Julia turned to Peter to apologise, but he did not seem to be able to look at her. He wheeled himself off the grass and away from the crowd.

"Well, that was certainly an *eventful* interval," Mary cried over the microphone. "But after spending time in this village, I'm not at all surprised. Shall we get on with why we're here? We still have a cheque to give away."

There was a grumble and a few people even '*whooped*', but the excitement level had been drained for the day.

"And the winner of the best garden in Peridale title, and the recipient of ten thousand pounds *is -*" Mary paused to fiddle and open a small envelope. "*Evelyn from the B&B!*"

There was a collective gasp, including one from Julia. Evelyn fumbled forward, her hands shaking under her kaftan. She looked back at the club, none of whom were clapping for her.

"We were taken by your garden's rustic charm and natural beauty," Mary exclaimed as Brendan handed the cheque to Evelyn. "I hope you'll spend your money wisely. C'mon, Brendan. We've done our bit. I need to get out of this village."

Brendan thrust the cheque into Evelyn's hands, and Mary dropped the microphone onto the grass.

They grabbed their things, scooted across the village green, jumped into a car and sped out of Peridale. Julia doubted they would ever return.

"I must say I am shocked," Evelyn said after scooping up the microphone. "I didn't foresee this at all. I prayed to my crystals, but the cards promised disappointment today. How *surprising!*"

She put the microphone on top of the speaker and walked over to the club, who quickly dispersed as they shook their heads and turned their backs on the winner.

"I couldn't have picked a better winner myself," Julia said after making her way back to the front of the crowd. "What will you spend the money on?"

"I've had my eye on a worldwide cruise for months," Evelyn said as she looked down at the cheque. "I'll spend the winter sunning myself on the best ship the world has to offer!"

"That sounds like a good idea," Julia said, looking around at the crowd who did not seem to know what to do. "*Right*, everyone. I didn't bake three hundred macarons for nothing! Let's tuck in."

CHAPTER 15

After a day of rest, Julia visited Emily in the hospital on Monday morning before opening the café. It was before official visiting hours, but a box of leftover macarons from the prize unveiling got her past the receptionist.

Emily had been moved from intensive care to her own room. When Julia knocked on the door, she was spooning yoghurt into her mouth. Her expression dropped, and her eyes widened.

"I'm not here to cause trouble," Julia said, producing the bouquet of red roses from behind her back. "I got these from Pretty Petals."

"My favourite," Emily said with a weak smile. "Pull up a seat."

Emily looked better than Julia expected. She had a bandage around her head, which squashed down her ears and grey hair, and her face was a little yellow, but she looked better than most would after a brush with death. She placed the yoghurt on the table and sat up a little more, wincing as she did. Julia put the flowers into an empty glass vase and helped Emily prop a pillow behind her back.

"I don't deserve kindness," Emily whispered. "I've been so blind."

"Everyone deserves some kindness," Julia said as she pulled a chair up next to the bed. "You're not a monster, Emily."

"I heard what you did," Emily said, turning her head to look out of the window at the pale morning sky. "I heard about you unmasking Mercy. That poor girl."

"She's looking at a lifetime behind bars."

"It's all my fault," Emily said with a croak, suddenly flipping her head back to Julia. "I wanted so badly to be in charge that I forgot about the people I was hurting."

Julia did not correct her. She did not want Emily to think she was getting off without some of the blame. Julia clasped her hand around her old neighbour's and gave it a reassuring squeeze. Emily smiled, and for the first time since that excited knock on the door with a copy of *Cotswold Gardening Magazine*, Emily looked like the woman Julia recognised.

"I can't believe Evelyn won," Emily said with a small laugh. "What she does *isn't* gardening. I don't even think she wanted to win."

"Maybe that's for the best," Julia said, letting go of Emily's hand. "If it wasn't for her giving Amy her special tea, I wouldn't have figured any of this out, and Amy might have died too."

"I feel so terrible," Emily whispered, a tear rolling down her cheek. "I treated my poor friend so badly. I treated them all so badly, especially Yolanda."

"You can't change the past."

"But I can change the future," she whispered with a firm nod. "I'm going to leave Peridale. How can I stay here? I've already called my son and told him to put my cottage on the market, so you're going to get a new neighbour. There's nothing keeping me here now that my roses are gone."

"Are you sure that's what you want?"

"I've always wanted to live by the seaside," Emily said with a calm sigh. "There's a little town on the south coast. Redwall, it's called. I have a cousin who lives there. Who says you can't have a fresh start at my age, eh?"

Julia clutched her hand again. She kissed Emily on the forehead and wished her good luck before slipping out of the room, leaving her to finish her yoghurt. She did not like to see Emily leaving the village, but a small part of her was relieved. She was not sure she would have been able to look her neighbour in the eyes every single day without remembering what she had done for the sake of a pin.

Julia drove back to the village and parked between her café and the post office. Just as she climbed out of her Ford Anglia, she noticed Jessie walking down the lane hand in hand with Billy. They kissed outside the closed Happy Bean coffee shop before Billy hurried off towards the cottage he shared with his dad. He saluted Julia with a wink as he passed.

"Is it safe to assume that he is your boyfriend

now?" Julia asked as Jessie walked towards her, hands in her pockets, and her hood low over her face.

"*Whatever*," Jessie mumbled. "How's the rose lady?"

"She's going to be okay." Julia pulled her keys from her pocket and unlocked the café door. "She's leaving Peridale and moving to the coast."

"Does that mean we're getting new neighbours?" Jessie asked with a roll of her eyes. "I swear to God, if they have any screaming babies or yapping dogs, I'm going to –"

"Morning, Julia," a man called from behind them.

Julia turned, her heart swelling when she saw Malcolm and Chloe walking towards the village hall.

"Morning," Julia called back with a wave. "Lovely day for it, isn't it?"

"It sure is," Malcolm called back. "Amy called me last night to arrange an emergency Green Fingers meeting to hand the pin over to me."

"Good," Julia said with a firm nod. "As it should be. You make sure to come into the café. I'll bake you an angel food cake to celebrate. You're both welcome."

Chloe smiled meekly from underneath her bob,

but she was not quite able to look Julia in the eyes. She figured it would be a long time before Chloe lived down the embarrassment of vandalising her neighbours' gardens.

As soon as all of the lights were turned on, customers flocked through the door, no doubt gagging to gossip after a quiet Sunday in the village. Julia and Jessie spent the morning rushed off their feet, so she was glad to see Barker when he came in for his usual lunchtime drink.

"Mercy has been charged," he said as Julia made him an Americano. "I hope the judge looks favourably on her because of what happened to her mother, but Johnny's evidence surrounding the obituaries proves all three murders were premeditated and it easily could have been four."

"It's Peter I feel sorry for," Julia said. "The poor guy has lost everything."

"I heard he's moving in with Malcolm and that Chloe is moving out," Shilpa from the post office said as she peered through the cake display case. "It's going to be a real bachelor pad."

"A happy ending then, I suppose?" Barker said with an unsure look as he accepted his coffee.

"Plenty more material for your book." Julia winked at him as she accepted his money. "I'm sure this ordeal would make a great sequel."

"You're writing a book?" Shilpa exclaimed. "How *wonderful!* Am I in it?"

Barker smiled awkwardly at her, his cheeks blushing brightly. Shilpa looked expectantly at him, but he was saved from answering when Dot burst through the café door clutching a magazine.

"Have you *heard* the news?" she cried.

"Here we go again," Julia whispered. "This is all sounding strangely familiar."

"*Look at this!*" Dot slammed the latest copy of *Cotswold Gardening Magazine* on the counter, which sported the headline 'Macarons and Mayhem'. "They've made us sound like *idiots!* There's hardly anything in here about flowers. It's all about how dysfunctional we are and how people should avoid our village! *Look!*"

Dot flipped through the magazine and landed on a page which showed Emily slapping the macaron out of Dot's hand. Julia was in the back of one of the pictures, her mouth gaping open as though she were catching flies.

"You said you wanted to be in a magazine." Julia was barely able to contain her grin. "Enjoy your fifteen minutes of fame, Gran."

Dot flared her nostrils and snatched up the

magazine. She hurried out of the café, slamming the door as she went. Julia finished serving Barker and Shilpa, and slipped through the beaded curtains into the kitchen. A tray of perfect macarons looked up at her from the middle of the counter.

"Where did these come from?" Julia asked. "These things are going to haunt me forever."

"I made them," Jessie said with a casual shrug as she washed the dishes in the sink. "Wanted to see if they were as difficult as you said. I don't know what all the fuss was about."

Julia bit into one of the macarons. She was more than a little surprised at how delicious and light the French dessert was.

"These might be better than mine," Julia mumbled through a mouthful.

"They *are* better than yours," Jessie said, flashing a grin over her shoulder. "I made them."

Julia tossed a tea towel in Jessie's direction before slipping back into the café. She stood behind her counter and stared out at the peaceful village green. The birds fluttered by while chirping their musical notes, the sun beamed high in the sky, and the hum of lawn mowers drifted in from a distance, bringing with it the pleasing scent of freshly cut grass. Everything was as it should be once again in

Peridale. Julia did not know how long it would last, but for now, she was going to enjoy it.

If you enjoyed *Macarons and Mayhem*, why not sign up to Agatha Frost's **free** newsletter at **AgathaFrost.com** to hear about brand new releases!

Coming August 2017! Julia and friends are back for another Peridale Café Mystery case in *Fruit Cake and Fear!*

Made in the USA
Middletown, DE
24 August 2017